Windows can't see anything. . . .

It was an old Victorian house on a large plot of land. But the lot was untended and the hedges overgrown. Above the gnarled and twisted shrubs the windows of the second story looked out on the street.

"Windows can't see anything," Jeff said. But even as he spoke the light shifted, and the house looked down at him with a dark, unblinking gaze.

Other Apple Paperbacks
you will enjoy:

Why Me?
by Deborah Kent

Nobody Listens to Me
by Leslie Guccione

A Cry in the Night
by Carol Ellis

Living with Dad
by Lynn Z. Helm

BEYOND the CELLAR DOOR

JAN O'DONNELL KLAVENESS

AN
APPLE
PAPERBACK

SCHOLASTIC INC.
New York Toronto London Auckland Sydney

With love, to Beth
who gave me the key

and for Pop
who growled always with love
1906–1988

ISBN 0-590-43022-X

12 11 10 9 8 7 6 5 4 3 2 1 6 3 4 5 6 7 8/9

Printed in the U.S.A. 40

One

Thwack! Grandfather's long finger struck, knocking Jeff's elbow off the table. The prop for his chin gone, Jeff lurched violently to one side, rocking the table as he scraped his fore-arm down its hard edge. His forkful of meat loaf shot past his mouth in a blood-red smear of ketchup.

"Settle down, Jeff," his mother said auto-matically, without looking up.

"Me? Why me? I didn't do anything. Tell Grandfather."

"Jeffrey," Mrs. Armstead warned. But her eyes slid past Jeff to the large, gray-haired man opposite her at the table.

"What did you do that for?" Jeff asked him, mopping with his napkin at the ketchup that dripped down his neck. "That hurt."

"It was supposed to smart some." Grand-father's glasses caught the light, hiding his eyes behind the bright glare. "Elbows do not belong on the dinner table."

"I was just resting." Jeff turned, appealing to his mother.

"Grandfather's right," she said. "Try to sit up while you're eating."

"You never minded before," Jeff muttered. He saw her cheeks flush, but she went on chewing and swallowing as if she hadn't heard him. "A person can't even relax around here anymore."

"Perhaps your head has gotten too big for you, Jeffrey, gained some extra volume," his grandfather said. "A swollen head requires a very thick neck or very strong shoulders to hold it up."

Out of the corner of his eye Jeff saw his mother's chin come up. She stiffened, straightening her back, and cleared her throat. Then Megan giggled. Perched on the edge of her chair across from him, Jeff's younger sister covered her mouth with a small, clean hand and giggled. Jeff chomped down on his meat loaf, swallowing it nearly whole.

"What's so funny about that?" he asked.

"Grandfather made a joke." Megan grinned at the old man in obvious approval. "But if Jeff really had a swelled head, Grandfather, it would float like a balloon. He'd have to hold it down, like this, not up."

She grabbed her ears and dropped her small

dark head between her shoulders, weighing it down with her fists. Her nose wrinkled and her eyes tilted, squinching up into black-lashed, almond pockets. Jeff felt the corners of his own mouth twitch. When Megan laughed, you couldn't look at her without smiling. Even Grandfather couldn't. But Jeff fought the impulse.

"That's funny? You're a real clown, Megan, a real clown."

"All right, both of you," Mrs. Armstead said. "Don't start. Jeff, wipe your neck. You look like your throat's been cut."

"Then all the air would come out, swoosh, and he wouldn't have a swelled head anymore," Megan said, erupting in giggles again. Grandfather's head bent toward her. His eyes were a bright, twinkling blue behind the lenses of his glasses, and at the corners was a crinkling of laugh lines.

"Right you are," he said to her.

Jeff's elbow was forgotten. His mother relaxed, the stiffness melting from her back, and smiled with Grandfather. Megan had that effect on people. At six years old she was already a diplomat. Unlike Jeff, she never got into trouble. Her shoes stayed tied, her hair stayed combed, and she never lost her papers, not once in the entire year of kindergarten. Teachers liked Megan. Amazingly, so did her classmates. Even Jeff couldn't stay angry with her, not in the face of her good nature and the smooth curl of her dark hair, not even over her annoying, absolute faith that she was welcome to follow wherever he went. Frowning, he burrowed into his dinner.

Eating at five-thirty was more like having lunch than supper. Besides leaving Jeff hungry again by eight, the early meal meant that the family ate with Jeff's father only on weekends. Commuting from Chicago, Mr. Armstead never got home before six-thirty. Until Grandfather came to stay, Mrs. Armstead waited dinner. Now she and Grandfather and the children ate early and went to bed hungry. Grandfather did not approve of evening snacks any more than he did of a late dinner hour.

"More pie, Dad?" Mrs. Armstead offered. "There's plenty left."

"Save it for Gene," Grandfather said. "And that means you, too, Jeffrey. No snitching your father's portion from the pantry."

"He couldn't," Megan observed. "We don't have a pantry."

"I wouldn't do that anyway, not Dad's." Jeff eyed the remaining pie. "Besides, there's enough for all of us to have seconds."

"Anyone can be tempted," Grandfather said. "Especially growing boys."

Jeff rolled his eyes back in his head, moving deliberately out of his grandfather's view. He speared his last bite of apple pie and reached for his empty glass.

"Pass the milk," he said.

" 'Pass the milk,' *please,*" Grandfather said.

"It's my milk. I don't have to say please."

Grandfather reared back in his chair. "What? What did you say?"

"Forget it." Jeff reached across the table for the milk pitcher. "I'll help myself."

"He didn't mean anything by it, Dad." Mrs. Armstead searched the table for a safe distraction, zeroing in on the coffeepot. "Would you like more coffee?"

"Thank you, no," Grandfather said and returned to Jeff. "I asked you a question, young man."

"I said, 'It's my milk.' " Jeff filled his glass slowly before he met his grandfather's eyes. "I don't have to say please."

"You most certainly do."

"Mind your manners, Jeff," Mrs. Armstead said in that quiet, warning tone. She set the coffeepot down. "Of course you say please."

"It s my house, not his. Why should I?"

"Because it's rude not to," she said, still quietly, carefully. "Besides that, Grandfather isn't just a guest here. This is his home, too. He's as much a part of the family as you are."

"More so, if you ask me."

"No one did." His mother brushed crumbs

from the piecrust off the tablecloth into the palm of her hand. They made a scratchy, abrasive sound in the silence. She studied them before she added, "But that's not the point. I expect you to be polite. You may apologize to your grandfather."

"For telling the truth?" Jeff swung around to face his mother. He could see the round o's of Megan's eyes and mouth, great dark pools of unhappiness opening wider with each exchange. "Since when do I have to apologize for the truth?"

"You let him talk back to you like that?" Grandfather asked. Mrs. Armstead didn't look at him.

"Jeffrey," she said. "Apologize or go to your room. We'll discuss this later."

Jeff shoved his chair back, hard, crashing it into the wall behind him, denting the wooden wainscoting. "I don't see why I have to eat with you, anyway. Why can't I wait until Dad comes home?"

"Somebody looking for me?" The screen swung shut behind Mr. Armstead. He strode into the kitchen, carrying with him the pungent smell of summer heat and automobile exhaust. They all looked at him, frozen for an instant like figures in a tableau. He was smiling, expectant, his face curled up like Megan's around dark eyes. Jeff had never before noticed how alike they were. Then the moment shattered, and everyone was moving, talking at once.

"Your son," Grandfather began, "needs a lesson in manners."

"Go to your room," Mrs. Armstead told Jeff. "Now."

"See you, Dad," Jeff croaked in an unfamiliar voice.

"Daddy," Megan wailed and threw herself at him. Mr. Armstead caught her up from her headlong rush, watching as Jeff bolted past him and took the stairs two at a time. Megan's short, plump arms clamped around her father's neck, and her face disappeared into the crook of his shoulder.

"What's going on?" he asked, bewildered by the sudden swirl of confusion around him.

Jeff didn't hear the answer. Upstairs he shut the door of his room on their voices, closing them out. He stood braced there, pressing his palms against the cool, white panels of painted wood, listening to his heart pound in his chest. It took a long time to return to its normal, steady beat. While it slowed and his breathing calmed, he remained spread-eagled across the doorway with his eyes tightly closed. At times like this he wanted to escape to the sanctuary of a time past, when this space was all his own. But when he looked, he did not see the remembered airy room of his mind's eye, with its shelves of model planes and walls plastered with posters of U2 and the Chicago Cubs. He saw the divided space, his retreat torn in half, and all his things crowded into the long, narrow portion that was now his.

"It's only temporary," his dad had said when he finished putting up the partition. "Megan can move back into her room when Grandfather gets settled. But for now, he needs a room of his own, Jeff. You can understand that."

It had already been a month, the glorious first month of summer. But instead of sleeping late or reading through the quiet mornings, instead of falling asleep to night baseball games, instead of planning projects to span the long vacation days of summer, Jeff had to consider Megan. She woke him early, and her earlier bedtime ruled out the radio. In his reduced space, there was no room for his elaborate building projects. Jeff glared at the partition. Just how temporary was temporary, he wondered? Another week? Three months? A year? He shuddered, and all his anger welled up again in his chest. When would Grandfather leave?

Two

"I don't know, Jeff. I wish I did." Mr. Armstead sat on Jeff's bed, his long legs bent in a tight Z that forced his knees up toward his chest. His hands dangled down, the fingers making spidery shadows on the floor. He watched them, frowning at their undecipherable hieroglyphs, as if they held the answers to Jeff's questions. "It would be easier for everyone, including your grandfather, if we had a definite schedule. You may not believe it, but this is as hard on him as it is on you."

"You're right," Jeff said. "I don't believe it."

His father looked up at him and smiled, a curling of his mouth that left his dark eyes sad. "That bad, is it?"

Jeff shrugged. "You ought to know. He's your father."

"But I don't know. You forget that he wasn't

around much when I was your age. I was Aunt Dorf's responsibility."

His father's childhood reminded Jeff of a Grimm fairy tale, so removed was it from the calm stability of Jeff's own. Gene Armstead's mother died just weeks after his birth, and his father left the newborn child with his sister, the formidable Aunt Dorf. Grandfather devoted himself to teaching and research, traveling all over the world. He returned regularly to visit his son, though he never stayed in town more than a few days. For years he had lived and taught in Europe.

"But what was it like when he came to see you?"

"I only remember what *I* was like," Jeff's father said. "Aunt Dorf would have skinned me alive if I'd misbehaved in front of him."

"I thought you liked her." Jeff pushed away from the door where he'd been standing since his father came into the room and sat down beside him on the bed. "You always said she was nice."

"She was, nice and strict. And she made the world's best chocolate chip cookies."

"The blue ones? Were they really blue chips?"

For a moment Mr. Armstead looked puzzled, and then began to laugh. "They were the only ones she took any stock in. That's a joke," he added, and explained. "My mother's family made lots of money on the stock market. They owned what bankers call blue chip stocks, good investments in strong companies. The Strattons thought I should live with them, because they could afford to keep me better than Aunt Dorf could. And Aunt Dorf, so the story goes, told them that the only chips a growing boy needed were the ones I could find in her cookies."

"Were they mad?" Jeff imagined a flour-dusted Aunt Dorf shooing bankers away with a rolling pin and a white dish towel.

"I doubt it. I wasn't much of a prize."

"Come on, Dad, seriously." Jeff grinned and butted his father's arm. Now that he'd turned eleven years old he considered himself too big for hugging, but he wanted the physical closeness, the comfort of his father's solid bone and muscle. "They must have really wanted you."

"I wouldn't bet money on it. I don't remember ever seeing them. Seems to me they moved away after old Mr. Stratton died. No matter, though. I grew up just fine on Aunt Dorf's blue chip cookies." He returned Jeff's grin with a real smile this time, one that shone in his eyes. "Welcome back. I was beginning to think you'd permanently misplaced your sense of humor."

Jeff sat up and glanced at the partition. "Wouldn't you?"

"We've all had our moments, even your mother and I."

"You're telling me," Jeff said with feeling. Then, at the look on his father's face, he tried to modify it. "I mean, Mom's been pretty grouchy, like a real artist."

"Your mother's worried about finishing her illustrations on schedule. This has been a big adjustment for us all, this new routine." His voice trailed off. "But I consider your grandfather's visit a very special opportunity."

Jeff sighed. Here it comes, he thought, the lecture on family responsibility.

"I'm not even going to tell you to stop me if you've heard this one," his father said, "because I know you have. I spent very little time with my father. Until I met your mother, Aunt Dorf was the only family I had. I had no idea what it was like."

"I'll bet you're sorry you found out," Jeff mumbled.

"Don't you believe it. I'd like to share my good luck with your grandfather. Why, he's practically a stranger to you and Megan. This is a chance for us all to get to know each other."

"He doesn't want to get to know me. He doesn't even like me."

"Of course he does, Jeff. You're his only grandson."

"And according to him, I'm no prize." Jeff meant it to sound clever, a twist on his father's own words. Instead it had a bitter edge. The sourness choked his throat and made his eyes smart with tears. "I wish he'd just leave me alone."

"Don't wish that," his father said quietly. "It's not the answer. I know."

"Why can't it be like it was, with just you and Mom telling me what to do?"

"Your grandfather has opinions and the right to express them."

"What about your opinions? Mom never disagrees with him."

"She doesn't know him very well, either, Jeff. And he's her guest, remember, a new member of the family." He reached over to the night table for a tissue and handed it to Jeff. "Look, I never said it was easy for any of us. But we all have to try to get along."

"All of us except Grandfather," Jeff said. "You don't know what it's like. You're at work all day."

"As your mother frequently reminds me," Mr. Armstead said, in a tone Jeff had never heard before. He looked up quickly, trying to read in his father's face what he didn't understand in his voice. But there was only a new tightness around his mouth and eyes as he met Jeff's eyes.

"I can't exactly quit my job to stay home," he went on, half to himself. "And civil engineers don't get paid leaves of absence to attend extended visits from relatives."

"There isn't enough room, anyway. Where would you go?" Jeff asked.

"Exactly," Mr. Armstead said, and some of the stiffness went out of his face. "In this house, we have to be a close family."

"It was big enough for the four of us." Jeff looked down again, at his portion of the floor.

"I know. But imagine how your grandfather feels. All his life he's lived alone. Finding himself in this zoo must be quite a shock." He smiled, but Jeff didn't look up. "I admit he's not an easy man. He's accustomed to having things his own way."

"What about our way? What's wrong with it? All he does is criticize."

"It's not that it's wrong, Jeff, but that it's different."

"You mean *I'm* different. That's why he can't stand me." He stopped his father's denial, brushing with both hands at the air between them. "It's true. Don't tell me it isn't."

"It's because he cares about you that he corrects you. You can learn all sorts of things from him if you listen."

"He never says anything to Megan. Doesn't he care about her?"

"You're older. There's less time with you." Mr. Armstead paused. "I grew up before he realized it. He doesn't want to miss his chance with his grandson."

"You can count on that. He never misses a

chance to tell me what I've done wrong."

"He knows a lot about the world."

"Not about my world," Jeff said, anger beginning again. "If he's not after me about my manners, it's my hair and my clothes. I like jeans. All the guys wear them. It's the style."

"But not his style," his father said. "Grandfather just wants you to look nice."

"I look normal at least, like everybody else. Besides, you told me not to judge by appearances. Why should he?"

"Try to understand, Jeff. He's been out of the country for years. Haircuts and clothes were different then."

"Can't *he* understand, too?" Jeff jumped up and went over to the double window that overlooked the backyard. "He never stayed this long before."

"It's past time he came home. There's a lot to settle now that he's retired. He has to find a place to live where we can keep an eye on him."

"Does that mean that you want him to stay here with us?"

"Only until he decides what to do," Mr. Armstead said. "There are financial arrangements to be made, legal affairs to settle, the property to deal with. Once he decides where to live, he'll have to get his things out of storage. Some of them have been packed away since my mother died. It will all take awhile."

"All summer?" Jeff asked.

"Maybe," his father answered. "We'll have to be patient."

"It isn't fair," Jeff said, his back still turned toward his father. In the silence he studied the long evening shadows cast across the lawn by the sinking sun. Voices sounded through the still air, distant but clear. It seemed a long time before his father spoke.

"No, it probably isn't fair. Lots of things aren't." His tone was sterner now, less conciliatory. "But that's the way things are. Your grandfather is not going to change the habits and opinions of a lifetime. We have to live with that as best we can."

"The rest of you don't have any trouble. I'm the problem."

"And the solution," his father said. "Control yourself and you control the situation."

"But Dad," Jeff began, swinging around to face him.

"I'm not saying that it's easy for any of us, or that you have to like it. I do expect you to treat him with respect." He stood up, slowly unfolding his long, lanky frame. "That includes saying please. Do I make myself clear?"

"Yes, sir." Jeff waited. "Is that all?"

His father reached out and rested one large hand on Jeff's head, tilting his face up. "You're very like him, you know."

"Like Grandfather?" Amazement won out

over dismay as Jeff considered that statement. "Me?"

"Give him time, Jeff, and yourself, too. You won't regret it."

"Yes, sir," Jeff said again. But his face remained set, his jaw still tight with anger. "Can I go out now, or do I have to say I'm sorry?"

" 'May I,' " Mr. Armstead corrected him and smiled. He hesitated as if he were about to say more, then shook his head and ruffled Jeff's springy, dark red hair. "No, I'll do the honors this time. You go on out and run off some of that energy."

Minutes later Jeff was on his bike, tearing down the flat straightaway of Grove Street. The big maples on each side rustled with evening, their heavy green leaves whispering in answer to the settling songbirds and plump gray squirrels. At eight o'clock it was still light with the cool contrasts of lengthening shadows and slanting rays of the setting sun. Jeff didn't think about where he was going, only about going there as fast as his bike would carry him, as if speed could burn away his anger. Automatically he followed his route toward school, to the playground where everyone gathered after supper to play baseball until the streetlights beamed yellow through the gathering dusk. He could hear the buzz of voices through the rush of air past his ears, voices that seemed to be calling his name.

"Jeff, Jeff, wait up."

He gripped the hand brakes hard and skidded to a stop at the corner, swinging the bike with him as he turned to look back. Megan was behind him, her short legs pumping as she raced to catch up with him. Her small bike, with its orange flag flapping high above her dark head, plowed like a bright red pinwheel along the sidewalk toward him. She stopped abreast of him, breathing hard, her cheeks pink with the effort.

"Where are you going?"

"I should ask you the same thing," Jeff said. "Mom will have a fit if she catches you out here."

"Not as long as I'm with you."

"But you *weren't* with me." Jeff looked back down the long blocks. "She doesn't want you crossing those streets alone."

"I won't be alone when we go back."

Jeff opened his mouth to shout at her and closed it again. It was pointless. No matter what he said, she'd follow him, and he was the one who'd be in trouble if he sent her back home alone. "All right," he said, wheeling his ten-speed onto the sidewalk. "Let's go."

But Megan remained still, both feet planted on the sidewalk on each side of the bicycle. "Are you all right?" she asked.

"Of course I'm all right. Why wouldn't I be? You coming or not?"

"You're not mad?"

Jeff sat up, straddling his bike. "Yes, I'm mad. So what?"

"At me? I was just trying to help." Her face was turned up to him, round and serious. "I thought if I made Grandpa laugh, he'd forget about you."

"No, I'm not mad at you," Jeff said after a minute. "It was a good try, anyway."

"You could make him laugh once in a while."

"Me? That old grouch? Let's forget it, okay? I've had one lecture already tonight."

But Megan still hung back. "Do we have to go this way?"

"It's the shortest," Jeff said. "If we're much later, everybody will be gone."

"Then let's cross the street."

"We'll only have to cross back at the corner. Come on, Megan, either come with me or go home."

"Promise you won't go too fast for me?"

"Let's just go. What's the matter with you?"

"It's that house, the one with the eyes."

"Houses don't have eyes," Jeff said, putting one foot on his pedal.

"Yes, they do. That one does." Megan pointed up the street to the house on the corner. It was an old Victorian on a large plot of land. But the lot was untended, and the hedges at its boundary were overgrown, reaching bushy heights of fifteen feet and more. Close to the house ancient rhododendrons competed with yew trees for space and light, shielding the lower floor from view. But above the gnarled and twisted shrubs the windows of the second story looked out on the street. Their blank glass caught the sun on either side of the center entryway. The gingerbread trim above the windows was peeling and gray, like bushy eyebrows above the staring panes of glass.

"Windows can't see anything," Jeff said. But even as he spoke the light shifted, and the house looked down at him with a dark, unblinking gaze. "There's nothing to be afraid of, Megan. Nobody's lived there for years."

"Is it haunted?"

"There's no such thing." Jeff watched the house. Once its clapboard exterior had been painted a soft rose, with gray trim. But the colors had faded, bleached, and peeled down to a patched and dirty white. The lawn was like a meadow around it, with clumps of cornflowers and Queen Anne's lace and milkweed growing in random spikes of color. Set back behind its heavy screen of hedge, the house stood undisturbed and unnoticed, silent and solitary. "It's just an old house."

"It's creepy," Megan said and shivered. "It looks like it's under an evil spell."

"That's your imagination. There are no spells and no evil magicians. It's just an empty house. See, the door's all boarded up. There's nobody there."

"It's still creepy."

"Not in broad daylight," Jeff said. "Nothing spooky ever happens in broad daylight. Let's go."

Together they pushed off down the sidewalk, past the thick hedge and hollow stare of the vacant house. Jeff kept glancing back over his shoulder, watching it recede as he pedaled slowly after Megan. Some angle of light made the whole structure appear to shrink with each foot he moved away from it and fade deeper into the soft evening. When he'd walked Megan across the next street, Jeff stopped and turned to look back again. Only the roof and turret rooms were visible now behind the barricade of bushes. Twilight blurred their outlines, as though the house were dissolving into the sky. Jeff blinked.

"Hold my bike," he said suddenly to Megan when they reached the curb. He ran back across the street to the boundary of the lot. At the corner he bent down and thrust his hands through a break in the hedge, parting the branches. He peered through. Once again the house loomed above him, pale and scabby with old paint, but solid. Its turrets beckoned to him. The windows gleamed down at him like yellow topaz, aglow with light. Jeff forced the stiff privet still farther back, opening a wider passage. He forgot Megan, his bike, the park, and ducked forward, wedging his shoulders into the prickly, fragrant shrub.

"Jeff? What are you doing?" Megan called to him, and the rasping leaves muffled her words. For an instant Jeff paused. Instead of stepping through the hedge, he looked back at her. The branches slipped out of his grasp and snapped together, scratching his bare arms and hands. Like a solid wall they cut off his view of the house. The thick green hedge hid it once more.

Jeff stood up slowly and rubbed his eyes. He hesitated for a moment before he withdrew toward the street.

"Funny," he said to Megan as he reclaimed his bike and glanced back one more time. "You'd think we'd have noticed that house before. But I never really saw it, not until now."

Three

Their silence as they moved to the side of his bed stirred Jeff out of his deepest sleep. His mother and father stood stiffly side by side, not touching. Mr. Armstead reached out and loosened the knot of bedsheet Jeff had clenched in his hand.

"Look at that fist," he said. "Jeff sleeps like he does everything else, with feeling."

"He's still angry. And I don't blame him."

"Liz, let's just forget it." Mr. Armstead straightened up. "These things are bound to happen, especially at first, until Dad gets used to us and we to him."

"That's just it. None of us is getting used to it." She spoke quietly, but emphatically. "It's been four weeks. How long does it take?"

"You sound like your son."

"I feel like my son," she retorted. "Don't you?"

"If you mean, am I angry? No. A little impatient, maybe, but I really think this can work."

"Because you want it to work, Gene," Mrs. Armstead said more gently. "I know how much it means to you to have your father here. I understand that at his age he needs to live near us. But he has to help, too."

"He just needs time."

"Meanwhile, it's like living on Mount Vesuvius, waiting for the next eruption."

Jeff twisted noisily in his bed, jamming his head under the pillow, wishing they'd stop. His parents never used to argue. He heard the soft hiss of his father's shush, the rustle of his mother's skirt as they left his room. But the dark peace of the night was shattered for Jeff. The lift and fall of his parents' voices pierced through his downy barricade as sharply as the light from their room cut across the hallway. And once again it was his fault.

"No, it isn't just that my routine is upset," his mother was saying now. "Although I can't understand why he doesn't realize that I'm working, just because I do it at home. I can live with that temporarily. It's that he doesn't make any allowances, and not just for Jeff."

Jeff heard the low rumble of his father's answer and opened his eyes.

"Yes, Jeff's usually the lightning rod for conflict, but even I can't win," Mrs. Armstead said. "If dinner's five minutes late, he wants to know why. It leaves him angry and out of sorts. Yet we're the ones who should complain. I lose half my working day, Megan and Jeff barely see you at all, and you have to eat alone."

There was another pause, another quiet comment, before she went on. "I don't care that you don't mind. *I* mind. The children mind." Her voice rose. "Couldn't we compromise a little? Eat early on the weekends when you're home and later during the week? Then you'd be here to talk to him."

"To Dad or to Jeff?" The bed creaked as his father got up. "I've talked to them both already. They're like match and tinder."

"But if you were here at mealtimes, Dad wouldn't focus so much on Jeff. Couldn't you ask him to consider it, at least?"

"We agreed on this when he came here, Liz. He's always had his big meal at noon. Five-thirty is already a compromise for him." Mr. Armstead's shadow fell across the hall from their doorway. "Why go over it again and again?"

"Because it doesn't work!"

"Can't you keep your voice down? You'll wake the whole house." Jeff's father closed the door with a thud.

Jeff slipped out of bed and closed his own door, trying to shut out the argument. He tiptoed to the corner of the partition and looked at Megan. She was lying sound asleep on her back, one arm crooked around her teddy bear, the other flung out to the side. She breathed deeply, with the soft bubble of an undeveloped snore, oblivious to the swirl of tension that had awakened Jeff.

If he concentrated on Megan's breathing and the hush of the summer night, he could push aside the other sounds. Like a bad dream they receded before the outside stillness. But it didn't make him any less responsible for them, he thought. If only he could learn to get along with Grandfather the way Megan did. If only he could learn to bite his tongue when Grandfather spoke, instead of prickling like a porcupine into spiny resistance. If only he could get used to Grandfather, and Grandfather to him, his mother and father could relax and things would return to normal. In the deep midnight quiet, it even seemed possible.

Jeff went over to the window. Leaning his elbows on the sill, he stared out into the backyard. Trees feathered a night sky sparked with fireflies. Crickets scraped creaky notes in the damp grass. A mosquito buzzed. Jeff pressed his forehead against the screen and strained to see as far as Grove Street, where that other house stood still and silent in its hidden yard. Behind its boarded windows its rooms were dark. But in the upper stories shadows moved at night along the walls and eased through half-closed doors.

In his imagination Jeff moved with them through the dusty quiet. What lay beyond its darkened windows, he wondered, kneeling at his own. As if in answer, images rose up of rounded, spacious rooms with skylights open to the stars, and cozy fireplaces, banquet dining halls, and kitchens big enough for pantries. So vivid were they that Jeff felt as though he'd actually been in the rooms. Finally, stiff but refreshed by the dreamlike visit, he stood up and listened.

The Armstead house was quiet, and no light showed from the hall. Jeff eased over to his door, opened it, and felt a rush of cool air from the window at the top of the stairs. At night the house seemed larger, as if, asleep, the family took up less space than in the daylight hours. Jeff yawned and stretched, suddenly sleepy, and climbed back into bed. Being awake at night was almost like being alone in his room again. He closed his eyes and let thoughts of the house on Grove Street lull him back to sleep.

But when morning came, everything was as cramped as before. The hall was just as narrow, and the house just as filled with Grandfather's presence. His gruff voice shook Jeff awake, jostling him out of the soft second sleep he'd drifted into after Megan gave up trying to wake him and left him alone.

"It's past time you were up and about,"

Grandfather called from the foot of the stairs. "Your sister's been awake for hours."

"I know," Jeff said. "I woke up, Grandfather, I just didn't get up."

"And why not?" Grandfather returned to the big armchair in the living room, to his coffee and newspaper, not waiting for an answer. He looked up when Jeff padded down the stairs from the bathroom.

"Don't you ever wear shoes?"

Jeff looked down at his bare feet and felt the familiar prickle attack his spine. "Yes, sir," he said and murmured to himself, "Control yourself, and you control the situation."

"What was that?"

"I said, I do wear shoes." Jeff turned to face him, wriggling his toes in the carpet. "But my feet like to be out on nice days. It feels good."

"It doesn't look good." Grandfather did not return Jeff's attempt at a smile. "You're not some hillbilly ridge runner who can't afford to be properly dressed. See that you put them on before you go outside."

"Yes, sir," Jeff said again. Maybe I need dimples, like Megan's, he thought, letting the smile drop as he escaped into the kitchen for breakfast. But there was no escape. He was standing in front of the toaster oven, poking a sharp forefinger into each cheek when Grandfather joined him.

"What's the matter with your face?"

"Nothing," Jeff said, jerking both hands down. Embarrassed at being caught redesigning his smile, he kept his eyes on the toast and his back to his grandfather.

"Your mother left you a note."

Jeff pulled the jar of peanut butter from the cupboard and set it on the table beside his plate and glass. He picked up the note.

> *Please drop Megan at the library for her story hour and discussion group on your way to practice, and pick her up on the way home. Make sure she brushes her teeth before you leave. And CLEAN YOUR ROOM.*
>
> *Love, Mom.*

"Rats," Jeff exclaimed, glancing at the clock. "That means I have to leave in fifteen minutes."

"That's not much time for cleaning your room and eating breakfast," Grandfather said. "Is that all you're having, that peanut butter?"

"I like peanut butter." Jeff sank his knife into the jar, and deposited a thick gob of the stuff across his toast.

"It's not much of a breakfast for a growing boy."

"It's high protein. If I put enough on, I can't even taste the whole wheat bread Mom buys." He bit off one whole corner and washed it down with orange juice. "It's all I need."

"Don't talk with your mouth full," Grandfather said. "If you got up with the rest of the family, you'd have plenty of time to eat a proper meal and do your chores."

"I'll have time to clean my room this afternoon, after practice."

"You'll clean it now."

"But Grandfather, I can't. I'll miss practice. And Megan's book program. She can't miss that."

"I'll take Megan."

"But," Jeff sputtered, "but it's summer."

"Summer is no excuse for laziness." The corners of Grandfather's mouth turned down so that long creases stretched between it and the sides of his nose. Fighting the insistent prickle of anger, Jeff took a deep breath. "Mom doesn't care when I clean my room, as long as I clean it."

The flat panes of Grandfather's glasses flashed at Jeff. "Don't try to get around me, Jeffrey. It's right here in black and white."

"It's also right here that I can go to practice." Jeff gulped the last of his juice. "You can ask her yourself if I can do it later. She won't mind."

"Good. We'll ask her right now." Grandfather snapped his newspaper sharply into folds and slapped it on the table.

"But she's working." Jeff's knife clattered off his plate, spattering peanut butter onto the tablecloth. He pushed his chair back. "You can't interrupt her unless it's an emergency."

Grandfather kept going. "She's only painting."

"She's got illustrations to finish, Grandfather, for a book. We aren't allowed, really."

He reached for the doorknob. "I can understand her not wanting you children to interrupt her every five minutes. But this is important."

"Can't you ask her at lunch?"

"By then it will be too late." Grandfather opened the door. "There wouldn't be any question about all this if you had an established routine."

"We have a routine," Jeff said. "At least we did have."

Grandfather glanced at him, and the creases deepened.

"I said I'd do it." Jeff darted ahead of the old man and flattened himself across the door of the makeshift studio Mr. Armstead had built for his wife in a corner of the garage. "It can wait."

"Putting chores off is no way to learn responsibility. I'm sure your mother would agree."

"Not right now, she won't."

"Don't be ridiculous, Jeffrey. Move. Whether you like it or not, we'll settle this now. You can't put me off."

"It isn't that, Grandfather, really."

"Then what is it?" He reached over Jeff's shoulder and unlatched the studio door. Jeff tripped backward with it, slamming the door into the shelves along the back wall, rattling cans of turpentine and linseed oil. A fat tube of titanium white rolled slowly to the edge and fell, landing with a soft plop at Jeff's feet. Mrs. Armstead jerked around.

"What on earth?" She had a wide paintbrush clamped between her teeth and a smaller one in her hand. "Jeff? What happened? Are you all right? Where's Megan?"

"We're fine, we're all fine," Jeff said quickly. "Sorry, Mom."

"I didn't mean to startle you, Liz, but Jeff refused to understand your directions. He's planning to go to the park."

"Yes, to baseball practice." Mrs. Armstead said, removing the paintbrush. "The town runs a recreational program."

"He's planning to leave before he cleans his room. I'm sure that's not what you intended," Grandfather said firmly, overriding her last words. "I've told him so, but he insists on hearing it from you."

"Yes, Dad, I see," she said, almost sadly, looking over her shoulder at the sheet of watercolor paper drying rapidly on her easel. "I am rather busy right now."

Jeff glanced up at his grandfather, a small

smile tugging at the corners of his mouth.

"You do expect him to clean his room," Grandfather said. His eyebrows ruffled together, and he seemed to lower over Jeff and his mother. "That's all I need to know."

She glanced again at the incompleted painting on the easel. "Yes, I suppose so, if he has time."

"He's to do it now, is that right? I want to be absolutely clear on this."

"All right, yes, now." Jeff's mother rubbed her forehead. She looked at Grandfather, and then at Jeff, who stared at the white tube of paint at his feet. She looked at her watch. "Where's Megan? She has to be at the library in ten minutes."

"Don't fret, Liz. I'll take her. I can help out around here. Now that Jeffrey understands what he's to do this morning, everything's under control."

"Thanks, Dad. You'd better go right away. She hates to be late." She dipped the brushes into a cup of water, swirling streaks of blue and green like bright banners through the liquid. They stood in silence, she and Jeff, until Grandfather was gone. After a while Mrs. Armstead sighed and lifted her head to look at the painting.

"It wasn't very good anyway," she said, tearing the sheet off.

"I'm sorry, Mom."

She sat down on the high stool by the easel and looked at her son. "What are we going to do?"

"Why didn't you just tell him I could do it later?"

"I don't mean about your room. Make your bed and tidy up before you go to the park, and do the whole thing thoroughly when you get home. I mean about you and Grandfather."

Jeff scowled down at his feet and tried to pick up the tube of paint with his toes.

"If you could try not to argue with him, it would help."

"I do try. He starts it."

"He's demanding, but surely you can find ways to agree with him once in a while."

Jeff looked up at her, hurt. "By giving in to him, the way you and Dad do?"

She closed her eyes for a moment, then opened them slowly. "Jeff, I want you to try to understand something. Accommodating your grandfather is not a surrender. This is not a war. His life has changed radically, and we want to help him adjust. It means a lot to your father." She paused, watching him. "Grandfather's work has been his life. Suddenly he isn't teaching; he's living in a country he abandoned decades ago, with a family he barely knows. After living alone he has to share this little house with four other people. His world's turned upside down."

"Dad said that."

"Didn't you listen? If you could help just a little more," she said, and her eyes flicked back to the rejected painting. "Do anything you can to make him feel at home. Maybe then he'll relax a little and it will be easier for all of us."

"Be like Megan, you mean."

"She does have a way with him, doesn't she?" his mother admitted. Then she smiled. "But you aren't Megan. You'll have to find your own way. Now go on, or you'll be late for practice."

Hanging from the handlebars, Jeff's mitt slapped against his knee as he raced down the driveway and headed for the park. Since he didn't have to drop Megan at the library, he had plenty of time left after finishing his lick-and-a-promise room cleanup. But he wanted to be well away from home before Grandfather returned. Not until he was out of sight of the house did he slow down. He turned onto Grove Street and straightened up in the saddle, letting the bike coast as he came abreast of the overgrown lot. He didn't have to think about whether or not to stop. His hands gripped the brakes, and his feet touched the ground involuntarily.

He was standing at the corner of the property where an iron chain was strung between two posts, spanning a neglected driveway. Strands of honeysuckle hung from the chain and clumped around the posts, twining up into the shoots of privet that grew out into the opening. Rings in the posts and the narrowness of the drive were more suggestive of horse and carriage than automobile, though clearly there had been no traffic of any kind for years. Stiff with rust, the chain creaked when Jeff propped his bike against it and stepped over it into the rutted driveway.

At closer view in the glaring sunlight, the house looked badly worn. Broken shutters hung askew at windows that were thick with grime. Bare board showed in spots through the peeling paint and gave off a not-unpleasant smell of sun-warmed wood. It was quiet in the yard, except for the scrape of Jeff's shoes on the gravel. He drew a deep breath, sweet with the scent of honeysuckle, and smiled. For the first time in a month, Jeff felt at ease.

In the long grass he spotted a faint path that led off behind the house. Jeff followed it as he would the crooked finger of a best friend into a deep, piney shade. The path ended abruptly at the base of a tall fir tree, where there was a broken stone bench on the edge of a brick patio. The patio was no longer level, heaved up by years of frost and thaw. Weeds were growing in the cracks, and bits of brick and shattered stone lay scattered everywhere. At its center was a cracked pedestal that might have held a birdbath or a silver reflecting globe. Jeff stepped forward to look and tripped on a piece of metal.

He picked it up, a small, calibrated arm in the shape of a triangle. Weighing it in his hand, Jeff looked at the chunks of marble at his feet. He shifted one with his toe, then dropped to his knees and shoved the pieces of stone around until they fitted together once more.

"A sundial," he said, grinning at the chipped face. When he set the metal arm at its center, he laughed aloud. In the deep green shade of the overgrown garden, it was utterly useless. "A lot of good that will do anyone here."

Mocking his words, the cracked dial reminded him of the time. "Practice," he cried. "I'll be late to practice."

And yet he didn't leave. Before he sprinted off to his bike, Jeff looked at the invitingly cool spot beneath the trees and brushed his hand across the face of the sundial. He snapped a stem of sweet grass and sucked it between his teeth, and breathed the warmly aromatic air. When he finally left, he took with him the touch and taste and fragrance of the yard that enclosed the hidden house.

Four

Hanging by his knees from a branch of the copper beech tree, Jeff could see all of the backyard, including the tomato patch that Grandfather was digging. Generally Jeff liked being upside down. He liked the idea of a green sky of lawn, and a cloud-tufted blue turf rooted with treetops. But from any point of view the garden meant only two things, both bad — no more batting practice with his father, and tomatoes. Jeff had nothing specifically against tomatoes, but if Grandfather planted them, he meant to harvest them. And that meant his visit would last through the end of the summer when the tomatoes ripened.

Jeff sighed and let his arms hang down, swinging them loosely in the cool shade. Batlike beneath the heavy canopy of beech leaves, he could see without being seen. He watched the regular thrust and bite of the spade as

Grandfather cut through the grass and turned up the black soil. Upside down in his farmer's overalls and straw hat, even Grandfather didn't seem quite so formidable. From Jeff's angle he looked shorter, more approachable. As he worked, his gnarled fingers flexed painfully around the spade handle. Every few minutes he straightened up from his digging and pressed the palm of one hand against the small of his back. At one point he paused, sank the blade deeply into the half-dug plot, and moved stiffly across the lawn to the house. Sunlight twinkled in the dew-damp grass and glinted off the windowpane as Grandfather opened the garage door and disappeared inside.

He could have asked for help, Jeff thought, and tried to imagine Grandfather's lips forming the words. Grandfather wouldn't know how to ask, any more than Jeff knew how to offer. Blood thudded in his ears, and he reached up, closing his hands around the gray bark of the tree limb. Lifting his head brought the world dizzily back to normal perspective, and he had an idea. He took a deep breath, hunched up against the branch, and somersaulted himself into space.

Jeff's feet pinwheeled over his head and he dropped to the ground with a thud, stumbling backward to keep his footing. He burst through the overhanging leaves of the beech tree, and came to rest on the newly dug earth.

The surface had dried already to a soft and crumbling brown, warm to the touch. Brushing off his hands, Jeff got up and pulled the spade free. Following the staked perimeter of Grandfather's plot, he began to dig. He tried to work quickly, to finish before Grandfather returned. As soon as the digging was complete, he'd disappear, leaving his anonymous gift behind.

The soil gleamed against the metal of the spade and crunched as Jeff forced the blade down. He could feel the hard edge of the spade under his gym shoe. Slowly the plot increased, and the square of green lawn became a lumpy surface of black clods. Jeff reached down and began to crumble them in his hands, raking over the soil with his fingers to smooth it as Grandfather's side was smoothed. He was hurrying now, one eye on the garage door. Pulling small rocks and chunks of roots from the dirt, he threw them backward toward the cover of the beech tree. He had nearly finished when his thumb caught in a narrow piece of chain. It lay close to the surface where Grandfather had dug and raked. From one end dangled a large brass key, an old-fashioned one with a long shank. From the other hung a round, flat disk. Jeff picked it up, shaking off the dirt, and saw that it held a snapshot, discolored with age and faded on the edges but still recognizable. It was a picture of a Victorian house, landscaped with low shrubs, light-colored with contrasting trim around the wide-open eyes of its upstairs windows.

Jeff stood up and stepped backward, forgetting in his surprise the spade he'd left planted at the edge of the plot. His heel caught its edge, and it jerked sharply downward, its handle smacking him on the shoulder as it fell. With his feet tangled in the handle, Jeff teetered off balance and pitched over on the grass, breaking through the string that marked the edge of the garden. He heard the crunch of something plastic, felt the spill of loose dirt and the rough hairy plant stems under his palms, and noticed the unmistakably acrid smell of tomato leaves. Half a dozen plants surrounded him, tilted at all angles on top of one another, scattered by his flailing as he tumbled over. Flattened beneath him were two pots, the plant stems still intact but the leaves crushed and torn.

Jeff sprang to his feet, still clutching the key chain, and looked toward the house. There was no sign of Grandfather, no movement inside the garage. Dropping the key into his pocket, Jeff straightened the undamaged tomatoes. For a moment he stared at the broken plants. Almost without thinking he snatched them up from their crushed pots and stripped off the torn leaves. Digging with his hands he sank them into the prepared garden plot deeply enough to cover the worst of their injuries. He swept the loose dirt from their pots into the grass, then sprinted with the broken pieces of plastic across the lawn to the garbage pails and dropped them in. From that distance the tomato patch didn't look too bad, its surface smoothed and even around the two short plants that still trembled in the sunshine with their sudden transplantation.

Breathing hard, Jeff brushed himself off and opened the door to the garage, heading for his bike. Grandfather was there, carrying the metal watering can and a box of fertilizer.

"Hi, Grandfather," Jeff said. He gave a small wave as he backed away. "Nice morning, isn't it?"

"You're going somewhere?"

Jeff nodded. "I've got to return something. It just turned up. I'll see you later, okay?"

Without waiting for an answer, Jeff jumped on his bike and pedaled off down the driveway. Looking back he waved again, and saw the blind glint of light on Grandfather's glasses as he watched Jeff ride away.

There were two possibilities, he thought, as he turned down Grove Street. Either Grandfather wouldn't notice the damage and would appreciate the work Jeff had done, or . . . or he would notice the damage. Jeff didn't want to think what would happen then.

He continued down Grove Street, the key

heavy in his pocket. As he approached the high hedges of the old house, he slowed and stopped. Where the front walk had once been the hedges had grown together in a sort of archway, leaving an opening only three or four feet high. Jeff peeked in at the front yard, then dismounted and ducked through the hedge, wheeling his bike with him.

The front steps of the house were hollowed with long-ago traffic, the boards split now and decaying. Loose shingles dangled off the porch roof, and the gray cone of a wasp's nest was visible beneath the eaves. The walk where Jeff stood was of flagstone, overgrown with weeds. He looked down the flaking, broken slates to the delapidated porch and up the peeling shingles of the house to the second-story windows. The blank panes met his eye. The lower turret room was closed and shuttered, and the windows of the one above it were powdery with grime.

Slipping the key chain out of his pocket, he looked at the pictured house again. He wasn't absolutely sure until he squinted, holding up the picture to match his view. Then he knew. It was the same house, certainly sadder than the one in the picture, but still the same.

Jeff rubbed his thumb back and forth over the brass disk and looked up at the bleakly staring windows. In the picture, with their pale curtains drawn back to each side, the windows had an air of mischief, a twinkle in the eye. Now they were mournfully black and empty. Their very loneliness appealed to Jeff, touching a chord of recognition deep inside him.

"I'm getting as bad as Megan," Jeff said to himself, shaking his head at his own fantasy. "She'd probably expect the door to open like a mouth and tell me how the key got buried in our backyard."

In spite of himself he glanced up, but the front of the house was shadowed and still. Nothing moved except the branches of the trees as the squirrels ran chattering above Jeff's head. Until that moment the difficulty of returning a key to an abandoned house hadn't really occurred to him. He glanced around for a mailbox and, seeing none, wheeled his bike up the path to the porch. Leaving it on its stand, Jeff picked his way up the rotting steps to the front door. Instead of a screen with a normal door behind it, there was a sheet of plywood padlocked over the opening. A no-trespassing sign was pasted to it, but it listed no owner's name or realtor's office. The windows, too, were not only shuttered but boarded over to keep out vandals. There was no exit from the porch at either end, where the shrubs grew thick beyond the worn railing. Jeff left his bike and walked slowly around the house through the tall grass and wildflowers.

Almost immediately he came to the wide side lawn and the remains of the brick terrace, bounded by azalea bushes. He noticed a wooden arbor he hadn't seen before, thick with late roses. Again Jeff felt the effect of the house on all his senses as it surrounded and gathered him in.

He continued on, past the back door, which was padlocked beneath a plywood panel that matched the one over the front door, and along the driveway side of the house. He saw the garage, a converted barn with its roof fallen in. But nowhere was there a place to deposit the key, or any indication of the owner's name. The heavy metal in his pocket tugged Jeff like a magnet toward the house, though he had not yet seen a lock that it would fit.

Just beyond the corner he came upon a sloped cellar door. Tilted at an angle to the ground, it opened up and out like a ship's hatch onto steps that led down below the house. Although the weeds here were high and the brush thick, they recently had been disturbed. The grass on the hinged side was flattened where the open door had rested on top of it. Curious, Jeff went closer. The door had a hasp fastener, with a combination padlock. The lock was new, contrasting with the rusted hasp, and had four numbers across its face. Often Jeff left his bike lock set with only one number of the combination out of order so he could release the lock quickly. He reached out and rolled the final digit of the basement lock up one. It clicked softly but didn't open. He rolled it down the way he'd found it and down once more. The lock clicked again and sprang open.

Jeff dropped it as if it were hot and jumped back from the door. He took a few steps away and glanced around, his heart pounding with sudden and irrational guilt, as if he'd just been caught breaking and entering. But the yard was empty and still, with birds and squirrels his only witnesses. In some amazement he stood for another moment staring at the open lock. And then his better judgment prevailed and his hand shot out, snake swift, to snap it closed again. But even as he spun the combination his mind recorded the numbers. With the key clanking in his pocket, Jeff turned and ran away from temptation and trespass. Retrieving his bike, he rode rapidly out of the yard.

"Where did you go?" Megan was sitting on the stoop waiting for him when he came home from the park for lunch. "Grandfather was looking for you."

"Was he mad?"

"Not at me," Megan said, her small face scrunching up in a grin. "Where were you?"

"At the park," Jeff told her. "What did he want? Did he say?"

"Before that," Megan said, ignoring his questions. "I saw you come out of the old house."

"Megan, what did he say?"

"Weren't you scared to go in there?"

Jeff kicked his bicycle stand down with one foot and swung off the seat. Experience had taught him that she wouldn't give up until he'd answered her. "So what do you want to know?"

"What were you doing?" Megan wriggled happily on the step. "Was it scary?"

"What's to be scary? I was just trying to return a key I found."

"You got a key to the house?" Her dark eyes widened. "You can get inside?"

Jeff shook his head. "It doesn't fit any of the outside doors. See?" He tossed the key to her. "It probably doesn't even belong there."

"But it does," Megan said, staring at the picture. "It must. Look, Jeff, look at the eyes. It's the house all right, only happier. Where did you get it?"

"In Grandfather's tomato patch," Jeff told her. "He must have dug it out of the lawn."

"Our lawn?" Megan looked up at him. "What was it doing there?"

"How should I know?" Jeff answered. "I didn't put it there; I only found it. Somebody probably dropped it there years ago, before our house was even built or something. Anyway, it's no good and there's nobody to return it to."

"Maybe it's the key to a treasure chest," Megan said. "Or a room full of precious gems and costly jewels, like in the fairy tales."

"It's not a castle in a story, Megan, it's just an old house in Arborton. Nobody around here has treasures." He smiled at her. "At least nobody I know."

"Mom has a jewelry box." But even Megan didn't sound too hopeful. "Still, I bet it opens a room in that house. And why would a room have a lock if it wasn't important?"

Jeff laughed. "Because it's the bathroom. That's the only room in our house with a lock."

"Can I keep it?"

"Of course you can't keep it. When I find out who owns the house, I'll give it back. Maybe I'll even get a reward."

"Just for a little while?" Megan asked, wrapping her small hand around the shank of the key. "Just until you find out?"

Jeff hesitated. "You won't lose it?"

Solemnly Megan shook her head. "I promise."

"I guess it doesn't really matter, as long as we have it."

"Thanks, Jeff." She launched herself off the step to grab her brother around the waist. "And can I help you find the owner? I'm good at finding things. Where do we start?"

"We don't start anywhere. I'll find out myself," Jeff said, unwrapping her. "Cut it out, will you, Megan?"

"You could find out if you went inside."

"You can't just go inside somebody's house, Megan. It's against the law."

"Not if you're returning something," she said, dancing away from him. "You aren't taking anything, you're giving it back. I'll bet you're just scared."

"I'm not scared. Besides, the house is all boarded up."

"Scaredy-cat, scaredy-cat," Megan chanted, giggling at him as she ducked around the railing of the front porch, dangling the key just beyond his reach. Jeff lunged after her and missed, sending her squealing through the screen door.

"Jeffrey?" Grandfather called out, intercepting him as he skidded into the front hall and headed up the stairs after Megan. "Jeffrey, stop chasing your sister."

"I'm not," Jeff said and regretted it immediately. There was no way now to avoid Grandfather, too late to pretend he hadn't heard, or that he was another of Megan's friends racing after her up the stairs.

"Then what are you doing?" Grandfather closed his paper and turned the sharp glare of his glasses on Jeff.

"Nothing, we were just fooling around, sort of." Jeff forced his lips into a smile. "Just playing."

"And were you just playing with my tomatoes? Come in here, please," he said before Jeff could answer. "I believe we have something to discuss."

Five

"He didn't even thank me."

"For what? Kneecapping his tomatoes?" Jeff's father sat across from him at the picnic table. The summer evening was fading into night, and the yard was blurred with lengthening shadows. "He'd want to nip that in the bud."

"Come on, Dad, it's not funny." Jeff concentrated on the mosquito that hovered and settled on his forearm, swatting it before it could draw blood. He flicked the corpse away. "It isn't as though I killed them."

"Lucky for you tomatoes don't object to having their leaves trimmed when they're transplanted." Mr. Armstead suddenly chuckled. "Of course, if you'd planted them all the same height, Grandfather probably wouldn't have noticed."

"He'd have noticed," Jeff said. "And told me

I did it all wrong. Everything I do is wrong."

"Not everything," his father said. But Jeff kept his eyes lowered and stared at his arm. "He was pleased that you dug up the patch for him."

"I'll bet."

"It was really thoughtful, Jeff, just the thing to do."

Jeff looked up. "It was?"

"Your grandfather hates to admit that there are some chores he finds difficult to do as he gets older. You made a hard job easier for him."

"You could have fooled me. How come he acted so mad then?"

Mr. Armstead smiled. "I used to ask Aunt Dorf the same thing. Why did he always look so mad when he came to see me? I thought I'd done something wrong."

"Had you? What could you have done?"

"Nothing. As Aunt Dorf said, it's a frightened dog that bares its teeth." His father mimicked his aunt's no-nonsense midwestern twang. "It didn't make much sense to me then. What she meant was that he was scared."

"Grandfather? Of you?"

"Less of me than of how he felt about me," Mr. Armstead said softly. "Some people can't show you how they feel, so they act angry to cover up. Your grandfather was always more at home with books than with people, at least after my mother died, ever since I remember."

He sat quietly across from Jeff, his face pale in the gathering twilight. His dark hair blended with the deepening shadows so that he seemed to be receding into the night. Jeff wanted to snatch him back from the darkness.

"And that's why he got mad at me?" he asked. "Because he couldn't say thank you?"

"Let's not totally ignore the tomatoes," Mr. Armstead said, leaning forward on the table. His closeness and the warm tone of his voice were reassuring. "The tomatoes had something to do with his reaction."

"I didn't have to tell him," Jeff said, looking at the dark square in the lawn where the six tall and feathery plants loomed above the two squatty ones. His voice edged into righteous outrage. "I could have lied."

"And I'm proud that you didn't. So is your grandfather."

"How can you tell?"

"He gave you full credit for admitting you were responsible."

"I could have told him I was working on a science project for next fall, about how planting tomatoes at different depths gets more or fewer tomatoes."

"Not a bad project, either," his father agreed. Then he said, more seriously, "I'm glad you told Grandfather the truth, even though he was angry. I know it wasn't easy for you."

Jeff shrugged, grateful now for the dusk that

settled around them and screened their faces.

"But," Mr. Armstead went on, "putting off telling him for two or three hours while you went to the park didn't make it any easier."

"Dad, he'd have killed me if I'd told him right away."

"You know better than that, Jeff."

"All right, not killed, but . . . I don't know," Jeff said, shrugging once more. "I just didn't want to be in trouble with him again. Everybody's always so mad all the time. I was only trying to help. It was an accident."

"Did you tell him that?"

"I tried. But he wouldn't listen. He never listens."

"That's not quite true, Jeff." His father shifted his position on the picnic bench. "He's just not used to listening to people your age."

"Or yours, either," Jeff blurted out.

"You might be surprised at how much he hears," Mr. Armstead said.

Jeff didn't answer. Then he suddenly said, "Maybe you should just divorce me."

"Where did you get that idea?" His father shook his head but didn't laugh. "Parents can't divorce their children. You're my son and you always will be, even when I'm as old as Grandfather. We're family. You're stuck with me."

"Then couldn't you send me to camp? Things would be fine if I could only disappear."

"We can't afford sleep-away camp this year, Jeff. And it would not be fine with me for you to disappear," his father said firmly. He tried a different tack. "Grandfather needs to be included in our lives, Jeff. If you invite him in, he won't have to bang the door down."

"I suppose."

"Got any better ideas?"

"I could just stay out of his way."

"As a temporary solution, that has its attractions." Mr. Armstead chuckled, gripping Jeff's shoulder with a warm hand. "But I hope you won't do that, not permanently, anyway. Besides, where could you go? You're too young for the Peace Corps."

"I don't know, Dad." Jeff thought suddenly of the quiet meadow of lawn and the drowsing house behind its thick green hedge. There was a place for him if he chose to unlock it. "I'll bet I could find someplace," he said.

"Running away never solved anything. Your problems are still here when you get back." He gave Jeff's shoulder a little shake. "I know you'll find a way to get along with Grandfather, gruff as he is. Is it a deal?"

Jeff hesitated, not sure he had a choice in the matter or any hope of success. "I guess so. I'll try."

"Good. What do you say we seal it in hot fudge? Get Mom and Megan. The sundaes are on me."

"And Grandfather?" Jeff got up, but stopped outside the back door. "Shall I ask him, too?"

"He's out on business tonight. Come on, before I change my mind."

By morning Jeff had his mind made up. He was already in the kitchen packing peanut butter sandwiches, apples, and a thermos of lemonade when his mother came downstairs. His father was still in the shower.

"Going somewhere?" Mrs. Armstead asked.

"Running away from home," he answered.

"Can I come?" She filled a mug from the automatic coffee maker.

"It's just for the day."

"Even that might help," she said and sat down at the table. No matter what time she got up, she eased vaguely into the day with black coffee and a view out the kitchen window at the squirrels in the cedar tree and the robins in the birdbath. Nothing much registered beyond the daily headlines until she'd been up for an hour or so. But this morning she looked more discouraged than sleepy. She blinked at him. "Where are you going?"

"Town Hall, and then maybe the library, and then the park, I guess, for lunch."

She blinked again. "Town Hall?"

"Never mind, Mom," Jeff said, easing around her chair toward the door. "I'll see you later, okay? I'll be home by five."

"Just don't be late, Jeff," she called after him.

At the center of Arborton was the village square with its band pavilion and war memorial. On one corner was the library, and facing it across the street was the Town Hall. Jeff was waiting when the clerk opened the door at nine.

"You'd have to request a search of the records for that information," the clerk at the property registry informed him. She looked at him with pale blue eyes over half glasses that pinched the bridge of her already thin nose. "And you have to have a good reason for making the request. A very good reason. Not just idle curiosity."

"But I need to know who owns the house on Grove Street."

"I am not here to entertain questions from small boys," she said, and the glasses shivered emphatically. "This office transacts legal business with adults, not children. ADULTS," she added, so that Jeff practically saw the capital letters. He left.

When the library opened at ten, he had no better luck. Ms. Sutter, the librarian, was willing to help but she was too young to remember who lived in the house Jeff described. The only book on local historic homes was already checked out, and the other references showed mansions on Chicago's North Shore. Ms. Sutter promised to research it further for him when she had time. By eleven o'clock Jeff was at the park, stirring up the dust under the swings with his toe as he drifted back and forth, thinking.

It took him a long time to decide on a plan, but finally he took his lunch and rode his bike back down Grove Street. He stopped outside the hedge of the old house. It couldn't hurt to look around once more, to see if there was any clue he'd missed to the identity of the owner. Still, he ducked nervously beneath the arched branches and wheeled his bike quickly up the walk.

In spite of the sun, the tall hedges and overgrown plantings around the house kept the yard cool. The stillness of noon was whispery quiet around him, even the birds and squirrels silenced by the heat. Vibrating up from the flagstones, waves of hot air disappeared into the green shade. The flat face of the house gave off a warm scent of wood from above the porch roof, and the eyes of the blank windows were wide against the raw sunlight. Jeff stood still for a few minutes in front of the porch, then walked his bike around the corner to the driveway and down toward the remains of the garage. He parked it out of sight beneath a mound of honeysuckle that climbed the sagging wall and made his way all around the house as he had done the day before, but in the opposite direction. He found nothing changed until he stopped at the cellar door, where the shiny combination lock lay face up in the sunshine. Once again it was set with only one digit out of place.

Jeff stood staring at it, the hot sun beating down on his head and burning through the thinness of his T-shirt. From somewhere beyond the tall privet hedge he could hear the greedy squeals of a noontime TV game show over the muted roar of a distant lawn mower. Cars passed by on Grove Street, their tires making a soft summer swish on the hot macadam. Nearer at hand were the occasional rustles of small animals in the shrubs, the click of a bike on the sidewalk. It all blurred together in the background, part of the world outside the still and silent house.

Jeff sat down on the peeling cellar door, opened his lunch, and took out half a sandwich. The cracked paint made a scritching sound under his sneaker soles and poked sharply through his shorts. He chewed thoughtfully, his tongue trapped in the sweet softness of sun-warmed peanut butter.

He wasn't worried about an unexpected confrontation with whoever left the lock. Whoever it was had returned to the house after Jeff had been there and had reset the combination before leaving. The fact that it was reset convinced Jeff that the house was vacant. There was no way to snap the lock closed from inside the cellar.

A slight breeze stirred the leathery rhododendron leaves, clacking them together and spreading the sweet scent of honeysuckle. Like a cool hand it brushed Jeff's face and lifted the hair from his forehead. Jeff leaned back against the house, against the warmth of the pale, weathered siding. As uncared for as it was, the old house retained its dignity and extended a gracious if formal welcome. Jeff felt himself relax in its sweet-smelling stillness. The tightness in his shoulders eased, and the constant knot in his stomach loosened. This warm silence held no menace. Far from being scared to go inside, he felt almost as though he were being invited. By chance he'd found the key and learned the combination to the lock, and the gentle peace of the house drew him to it. As Megan said, it wasn't as though he wanted to take something, or even to snoop around. He wanted to return the lost key. Swallowing the last of his sandwich, he picked up the lock and let it rest in the palm of his hand.

The sign said no trespassing. But was he trespassing if he had a key? Surely it could do no harm to explore now, while the house was empty. Since he didn't plan to disturb anything, since his mission was, in fact, to the owner's benefit, he couldn't see that it would be wrong. Quite possibly his entry wouldn't even be noticed. Jeff put the lock down again and thought about it while he drank his lemonade. But the idea was now irresistible. Decided, he repacked his sandwich papers and thermos in the bag and shoved it into the weeds beside the cellar door. As soon as he slipped the numbers of the lock into the remembered order, the hasp clicked open. Jeff slipped it off, lifted the latch, and swung back the door.

The cellar exhaled a strong breath of damp darkness, in contrast to the sunny warmth of the yard. Jeff looked down a slanted stone stairway with a rough wooden banister on one side, into blackness. Only the upper steps were visible in the shaft of sunlight through the open door. It smelled musty, cool and earthy. Jeff bent down to see where the stairs led, but it was too dark. After a minute he straightened up and ran back to his bike. He removed the headlamp and returned to the cellar. Glancing over his shoulder at the empty yard, he laced the lock through the latch of the door and snapped it to, then pulled the door shut behind him as he edged down the stairs.

Only a sliver of light came through the unsealed doorway behind him, cutting faintly through the darkness before it was absorbed by the deep shadows. Jeff switched on his light, but it was little more than a glimmer in the thick blackness. In spite of himself he shivered as he made his way slowly to the bottom of the steps. Here he swung the torch in a wide half circle and let it play over the walls and ceiling of the cellar.

The ceiling was surprisingly low, supported by roughly hewn beams, dark with age. Where he could see them, the walls appeared to be brick, fuzzy with dirt and grime. If there were windows, they were tightly shuttered and allowed no light into the dim foundation of the old house. On each side of the steps was a clutter of odd shapes — boxes, chunks of lumber, thick arms of pipe, and mysterious draped masses. By aiming his light directly onto the floor in front of him, Jeff could make his way among them without tripping or hitting his shins. Head down, he moved slowly with the light in one hand, the other extended into the darkness. The scuff of his heels reverberated like the tread of a ghostly companion. He touched nothing, yet the shadows seemed to rustle around him as he passed. Straining to see, he moved more deeply into the maze, all his senses on edge. Something brushed by his left ear. Before he could push the image of flitting bats from his mind, a slightly sticky, velvety stroke fluttered at his cheek.

"Get away," Jeff shouted, swinging his light wildly as he leaped backward. But where there had been space behind him before there was none. He came down hard on something soft, something that pulled away with a sharp cry. Jeff lurched to one side and felt beneath his fingertips the unmistakable texture of human skin.

Six

"Megan?" Gripping the light in both hands didn't keep them from shaking, Jeff discovered as he pointed the flashlight beam at the small shape on the floor at his feet. "What are you doing here? How did you get here?"

"I saw you from the corner," she answered, blinking back tears of terror. "I saw you come into the yard, and I followed you."

"You couldn't have followed me." Jeff crouched down in front of her and wiped at her face with a corner of his shirt. "I'd have seen you."

She shook her head. "I came up the front walk, and when you went back to your bike for the light I ran down into the cellar. You scared me," she wailed suddenly.

"*I* scared *you*? What do you think you did to me?" He bent close to look at her. "Hey, it's all right. You aren't hurt, are you?"

"No," she said, her voice wobbling. Reaching up, she took Jeff's hand and held it tightly. After a few deep breaths her face relaxed and her mouth curled slightly, returning to its more cheerful contours. "Weren't you scared to come inside?"

"Not until you came along," Jeff said.

Megan managed a full smile. "But you were scared then."

Instead of answering, Jeff turned the flashlight away from his sister and let the beam play along the ceiling and the pathway where he'd been walking. Hanging from one of the beams was a swag of cobweb, caught together on itself like a dusty piece of lace.

"That's what scared me," he said, shining the light on it. "Then I ran into you."

"You sure did." Megan massaged her foot. "What do we do now?"

"We?" Jeff swung the flashlight toward her. " 'We' don't do anything. I try to find a clue to the owner of this place. You go home before Mom skins you alive."

"She'll skin you if she finds out where you've been."

"But she won't find out, will she, Megan?" Jeff focused the light on his sister's face. "You wouldn't dare."

"Tell her? Not if I'm helping you, I wouldn't." Brushing herself off, she stood up. "Where do we start?"

"That's blackmail." Then Jeff decided on a different tactic. "It's not going to be any fun. You don't want to poke around dirty old cellars. I'm only going to glance inside, if I can get in. I'm not staying."

"I'll help."

"You'll just be in the way, Megan. What can you do?"

"Unlock doors." She reached in her pocket. "I've got the key, remember?"

In fact, he had forgotten. When Jeff left the house that morning, he didn't plan to enter the old house, only to investigate it and discover who owned it. Now, as Megan dangled the key in front of him, he realized that he might need it. But short of snatching it out of her hand and dragging her bodily out of the cellar, he was not likely to get the key without letting Megan come with him.

"All right, then, come on. But stay with me and don't touch anything."

With Megan clinging to the belt loop of his shorts, Jeff began again to pick his way across the dark cellar. Knowing it was Megan's footsteps that echoed his own made the journey less ominous, and by the time they came to a doorway on the far side of the cluttered room, Jeff had regained his calm. Now that his eyes were accustomed to it, the cellar didn't seem quite so dark. He found the door handle easily and turned the knob. The door swung back.

This time it was Megan who crashed into Jeff. He stopped short, gasping at the thing that rose in front of them. For an instant, under the watery glimmer of his light, it seemed to move toward them, open-mouthed and multiarmed, silently reaching out to snatch them up. The flashlight jerked in his hand, and his voice caught in his throat as he shoved Megan backward toward the safety of the crowded room they'd left.

"What is it? What's the matter?" she cried as Jeff stumbled into her, his light flashing crazily over the shadowy gray shape in the center of the room. Its limbs writhed soundlessly beneath the shifting patterns of light and dark. Scrambling backward, Jeff thudded into the doorjamb, his escape momentarily blocked. The light steadied, the shadows cleared. With a rush of relief Jeff leaned against the doorway and laughed weakly.

"It's all right," he said, laughing again. "It's just the furnace."

The burner filled the room, a great cylindrical tank with ducts like arms growing from all parts of its body. Squatting in the center of the room, it resembled a primitive icon, clumsy and industrial, raising its metal appendages to an unnamed god.

"It looks like a monster," Megan whispered, awed. Two gauges jutted out like eyes on stalks, and a metal door in its belly might have been a mouth, ready to devour anything within reach. A black throat yawned beyond Jeff's light, and dust dribbled hungrily through the grating to the floor. "It's even got teeth."

"That's just the firebox, where you shovel in the coal," Jeff told her. But he lowered his voice, too, as if the ugly giant could be awakened. He heard a stirring of the silence above their heads — a soft brushing of velvety fingertips, a drifting of dust in the air. He moved the light and heard it again, a drowsy rustle overhead. It raised the hair on his neck, and the skin of his forearms prickled into goose bumps.

"What's that noise?" Megan asked, pressing up against him. "It sounds like baby birds."

"But it's not, not birds." Again Jeff pushed her back through the door. Grime crunched beneath his feet, dry and crumbling. His light skimmed the floor and its litter, showing the scrapes of other footsteps, then touched the body of the old furnace and trembled upward into the mass of flues. Like gray sea serpents the ducts coiled and twisted into the walls and floors of the old house. Small dark shadows seemed to flutter away from the pale reach of the beam, and the rustling increased. Jeff shuddered. "Let's get out of here."

He pulled the door shut behind them, making sure it latched, and ran his free hand through his hair and down the back of his neck. "Go on, Megan, move," he said, urging her back toward the cellar exit.

"You don't have to push. What's the rush?"

"You'll rush if those bats come swarming out after us." Jeff rolled his shoulders at the thought of the small, flitting beasts filling the air around them. "Come on."

"Wait, wait for me," Megan cried, trying to rub her hands through her short, dark hair and still hang on to Jeff's belt loop. "Where are you going?"

"Where do you think? I'm getting you out of here." Jeff swung the light back toward the cellar entrance. "You can wait for me outside."

"What about you?" There was a drag at his back as Megan slowed down, controlling her panic.

"I'm going upstairs. But one more surprise like that, and I'll be right behind you."

"It's not true what they say, is it?" Still brushing at her head, Megan stopped short. "Bats don't get caught in your hair. They have radar."

"Sonar, actually," Jeff said, pointing the flashlight to the cellar steps. "I'll see you in few minutes."

"Promise you won't stay?" When he nodded, Megan squared her shoulders and tucked her small hand into his belt loop again. "Let's go then. I'm coming with you."

This time Jeff didn't bother to argue with her. He was as eager as she was to get out of the cellar with its dark, invisible rustlings. Zigzagging through the dimness, he led them to a set of stairs on the far side of the cellar. The boards were hollowed with use and creaked when Jeff put his weight on them. Testing each one, he eased up toward the door at the top.

"Suppose it's locked," Megan asked.

"We'll try your key," Jeff whispered back. But when he wrapped his hand around the knob and turned, the door creaked back on rusty hinges.

The room into which they stepped was nearly as dark as the cellar they'd left. Louvered wooden shutters were closed over the windows, and these were boarded across on the outside. Motes of dust floated in the bands of light, giving the kitchen a hazy, golden zebra stripe. Dim cliffs of counters and cupboards hung from the four walls, and a table straddled the center of the floor. Abandoned on top of it was a vase of flowers, dried long ago to brittle brown, lit by a single delicate ray of sunshine.

"Look, Jeff, the house is glad we came." Megan ran over to the table. "It's a welcome bouquet."

"A dead bouquet," Jeff said, wrinkling his nose. "Whoever lived here must have left them."

"They're dried flowers." Kneeling on a chair Megan pulled the vase toward her. "Strawflowers and baby's breath . . ."

"And dust. Leave it alone, Megan, it's filthy like the rest of this place."

Dust layered all the surfaces, muffling the kitchen with the undisturbed weight of the past. Even the light was stained with it. An old-fashioned gas range, once the majestic heart of the room, huddled beneath its grime. The cupboard doors were hinged with cobwebs.

"Looks like nobody's been here for years," Jeff said, running a finger across the drainboard. Dirt clung like gray suds to the sink. A small brown spider rested at the center of the web he'd spun between the faucets. "What a mess," Jeff said and sneezed.

"Let's clean it up." Megan held the vase in front of her and blew, adding a tornado to the specks that drifted in the beams of pale light. "Then somebody might buy the house and move here to live, somebody with children my age."

Jeff sneezed again. "Would you put that down? I said not to touch anything. We're not supposed to be here, remember? And we aren't cleaning anything up."

"It would be like in the fairy tales," Megan said. "Like magic, the house would be all beautiful again. Besides, how are we supposed to find clues if we don't touch anything?"

"Just look around, and be careful." He pulled open a drawer next to the sink. Odd pieces of silverware, a can opener, and a rusty fork rattled together. The cupboard beneath the drawer held only a rusty skillet. "Look for something with a name and address on it."

Megan leaned one hand on the table and set the vase carefully back where it had been. Sliding down from the chair she began to inspect the cabinets on her side of the room. They were empty. She moved from one to the next, flipping open the doors.

"Jeff, here's something. I've found something. Look." Flapping on the cupboard door was a calendar. "It's years old, though."

"That doesn't matter." Jeff flashed his light over the faded dates. " 'Dentist appointment, car repair, movers,' " he read, following the weeks in a long-ago July. But when he turned to August, the notations stopped. September and October were blank, and November and December.

"They moved, I guess," Megan said, losing interest. "Aren't you thirsty? Want a drink, Jeff?"

Before he could answer, Megan swung around to the faucet. It coughed and belched when she turned it on, and suddenly a stream of water exploded into the sink, swirling the dust and dirt down the drain. It exposed the sink's white porcelain in a sudden sunburst pattern. Jeff stared at it.

"The water's on," he said.

"It's a faucet, isn't it?" Megan slurped water from her palm to her mouth. "What did you expect?"

"No one lives here, Megan. Abandoned houses don't have water, or electricity. There's no one to use it." Jeff looked up at the round white globe on the ceiling. Beside the doorway nearest the sink was a switch. He pressed it, and light filled the kitchen. He and Megan stood still in the sudden brightness.

"I think we'd better go," Jeff said.

"But we haven't found any clues. And I like it here. I like it lots better with the lights on. Come on, Jeff, let's explore." She wiped her palm on her shorts and dried her mouth, leaving a grimy mustache on her upper lip. "Don't just stand there. What about the clues?"

"There are plenty of them," Jeff said. "Footprints, fingerprints, no one could miss them. You'd have to be blind not to know we were here."

"So what? Who's looking?"

But Jeff was thinking about the running water, the lights, the shiny new lock on the cellar door. "I don't know. But someone will be."

Megan's smile slipped. In spite of her mustache she began to look worried. "You're just trying to scare me so I'll go home. But I'm not leaving until you do."

Jeff turned to look over his shoulder at the door to the cellar. "Did you see anyone outside? Could anyone have followed you when you came in?"

"You can't scare me," Megan said stoutly, her small hands gripped in tight fists by her sides. "There was nobody outside but you."

"You followed me," Jeff said, still staring at the door.

"Just stop it, Jeff Armstead." Megan stamped one small foot. Her forehead wrinkled in a frown that barely hid the trembling of her lips. "There's no one here except us."

"Not now," Jeff said. He stepped forward and shot the pin of the dead bolt he saw on the door. "Still, there's a chance someone could show up."

"Who?" Megan relaxed a little once the door was locked. "Who'd come here?"

"Whoever put the new padlock on the door. And we could be in a lot of trouble if whoever that is found us here."

"We're just returning the key." Megan gave him a wobbly and deceptively innocent smile. "There's nothing wrong with that."

"Maybe not," Jeff said. In the bright light their footprints stood out on the dusty floor. Megan's palm print was clear on the kitchen table, his own fingerprints smeared on the countertops. "But just in case, let's work a little of your magic. Better to clean the place up than to leave our tracks everywhere."

In the pantry they found what they needed. There was a dented tin bucket, a threadbare string mop, and a broom with a handle broken at exactly the right height for Megan. While Jeff wiped down the cobwebs, Megan attacked the floor, sweeping up the dirt and trash. Although the house was shaded and cool inside, the air was stale and lifeless, closed off for too many years behind the sealed shutters. Warmed by their work, Jeff and Megan unlatched the windows and shoved them open to whatever fresh air could find its way through the boards and broken louvers of the old wood.

They filled the sink with water and sluiced down the countertops. Using Jeff's T-shirt, they scrubbed the tabletop until the butcher block surface gleamed in the electric light. Megan polished the glass vase on the tail of her shirt, and rearranged the flowers before she replaced it on the table.

"Now it feels like home," she said. "You're glad to shake off all this dust, aren't you, House?"

"It isn't alive, Megan, like a dog that needs a bath." But Jeff felt it, too, a different texture in the kitchen. Where the dust had swallowed and dimmed the light, the clean counter and stove top reflected it in small twinkles and flashes. The cut glass of the vase prismed the tiny shaft of sunlight and cast it into rose and purple fragments on the floor. Even the slight movement of summer air gave new vitality to the room.

"It may have windows that look to you like eyes," he added, "but the house doesn't have ears."

"Then what's this?" Megan reached up and took a cone-shaped object from its hook on the wall above her head. A hollow tube ran from it to a wooden plate on the wall. Holding the cone to her mouth, Megan said, "Hello, House, this is Megan speaking. How are you today?"

"You don't expect it to answer, I hope," Jeff said, watching her hold the cone to her ear.

She shrugged. "What is this? It looks like half a telephone."

Jeff took it from her, peered into it, and held it to his own ear. He heard nothing but the rush of still air.

"It's not a phone," he said, since it had no wiring and no bell or dial. "I know. I'll bet it's one of those speaking tubes, the kind they had in old houses to call the servants. You blow in one end, and start talking, and the butler, or in this case the cook, can hear you in the kitchen."

"Then it is a phone, a house phone. I can talk to the House." Megan giggled, but took the tube back from Jeff and, standing on tiptoe, continued her conversation. "I'm glad I came today," she said. "It was nice of you to leave the flowers in the kitchen, even if they were sort of dusty. Your water was delicious, but lemonade and cookies would be nice, too. Jeff likes chocolate chips."

"You're crazy," Jeff said, snatching the tube out of her hand. "Next thing you'll be ordering roast beef."

"No, peanut butter and jelly. I'm hungry."

"Good. Go home. It must be close to dinnertime."

"We haven't even seen the rest of the house," Megan said. And without waiting, she pushed open the swinging door out of the kitchen.

Seven

"It's a roomful of tents," Megan cried and darted forward. In the shuttered gloom the draped furniture did look like tents, a whole encampment of them. All along the walls and beneath the bay window were covered shapes of varying sizes, yet the huge room sounded hollow and empty. Even the biggest tent, in the center of the room beneath a dusty chandelier, did not crowd the cavernous space.

"It's the dining room." Jeff propped the door open and stepped across the threshold after his sister. "They must have left the furniture here."

"Where else could they go with it? Where else would it fit?"

"Not in our house, that's for sure."

"Let's see what it looks like." Megan slipped past Jeff. Reaching up, she pulled on the heavy velvet that curtained the windows. A shower of dust and flaking paint sprinkled down. "Ugh," she said, wrinkling her nose. "These could stand a washing."

"Haven't we done enough of that today? Leave them alone." Jeff turned his flashlight on the walls. They were marked by squares and ovals where pictures had hung. He flicked the light up. "Look at that ceiling."

High above their heads plaster designs swirled like icing on a cake. Edging the walls was an elaborate molding of twisted vines and flowers. At the center of the ceiling was a huge medallion, its garlands bursting in high relief around the base of the crystal chandelier. In spots, chunks of plaster had broken and fallen into dusty powder on the floor. But the moving shadows of Jeff's light gave the illusion of motion, as though a fresh breeze were passing through the lifeless, eternally still leaves.

"I still can't see." Megan grabbed the tarnished gold braid of the velvet hangings and pulled them back. With a soft sigh the material parted and shredded away from the curtain rod, falling with a thump that raised a cloud of dust at Megan's feet. A shaft of sunlight needled through the partially unveiled windows, angling between the broken louvers outside to strike the chandelier. Even through its layers of grime the crystal caught the light and splashed it around the room.

"Diamonds! I told you there was treasure in this house."

"It's just glass, Megan." Jeff touched the light switch, but only a few of the bulbs in the chandelier lighted. Festooned in cobwebs, it shone feebly, as though it were wrapped in dingy gauze. In the artificial light, everything looked shabbier, more dilapidated than it did in the natural half-light. "Come on," Jeff said. "Let's get out of here before the ceiling caves in."

"What about this?" Megan prodded the rotted velvet with her toe. "Shouldn't we hang it back up?"

"Never mind," Jeff said. "It could have fallen of its own weight, it's so worn out. Just leave it. Let's go."

"I want to see the furniture." Megan lifted a corner of the canvas beside her, revealing a long chest with an elaborately carved front. She dropped to her knees and ran her fingers over the dark, smooth, wooden shapes. "There's a unicorn and a castle. It's like a story."

"We haven't got time for stories."

"Look, it's got feet." Megan pointed to the base of the chest. Short legs, fashioned like claws gripping glass globes, held it up. "Do you suppose the table and chairs are like that?"

"How should I know?" Impatiently Jeff shifted from foot to foot, flashing his light into the dim corners. "Come on. We haven't got all day."

"Wait up. We haven't looked here yet." Megan yanked on the door of the chest, but it was either locked or stuck tight. Jeff hesitated. At the edges of the room the floor was bare, dark with age and stained by years of neglect. At the center was a worn cocoa matting. Megan was kneeling on it, and he could cross the room on it without leaving footprints behind in the dust of the floorboards.

"All right. You stay here and see what you can find. I'll check the rooms across the hall."

The dining room opened onto a large hallway, with glass doors separating it from the front entrance. An Oriental carpet ran down the hall and off toward the staircase to the upper stories of the house. On the far side of the hallway was another doorway, a square opening flanked by wooden columns that matched those in the dining room.

It's the parlor, Jeff thought, jumping from the matting to the carpet. Like the dining room, it was a big room with bay windows at the side and front of the house. It, too, was shuttered, the darkness intensified by the thickness of the overgrown shrubs outside. The furniture was gone, and the carpeting. Only tatters of matting lay on the floor. Jeff hopped from one to another, as if they were stepping stones in a wide, black river. His breathing echoed in the still room, bouncing off the hard, bare walls and ceiling.

Pausing to look around, Jeff saw a marble fireplace angled into one corner. At the far end of one of its walls was a double door, its woodwork carved in the same pattern as the mantel. There was a long, shanked key in the lock.

It's just like the one I found, Jeff said to himself, reaching out for the key. It came easily out of the lock, an old-fashioned heavy design that matched the one he'd given Megan. Jeff closed his fist around it, then replaced it in the lock and opened the door.

The warm, stale air could not hide a lingering scent of books in the empty room — of paper and ink and thick, gold-stamped bindings. The bare shelves lined the walls from floor to ceiling, dusty and still, yet expectant.

It was the first library Jeff had ever seen in a private home. Its shelves had once been filled with books and other treasures. But the room wasn't grand or imposing. Immediately he felt at home in it. The long arms of its shelves reached out to him, offering comfort. Though it was small in comparison to the rest of the house, the room gave an impression of lightness and space. If this were his home, Jeff knew it would be his favorite place. The richness of the wood, the cheery warmth of the tiny fireplace in the corner, the whisper of silence that was like the ghostly turning of pages long gone — everything about this room appealed to Jeff. If he could stand here for even a minute each day, he thought he could bear the cramped unhappiness of his own home.

It was a waste that the room was empty. Forgetting the tracks he might leave, Jeff wandered about the library. He touched the bookcases and noticed how the setting sun had bleached their western edges. He bent over the fireplace and held his hand over the cold hearth and felt warmed. He lingered at the glass-fronted cabinet, swinging the doors up and down on their tiny brass hinges.

"I'd put my planes here," Jeff whispered, smoothing his hand across the wide shelf. "I could start a real collection of models and have a place for all of them."

The room expanded around him as he imagined it filled with books about planes, as well as his own favorite adventure stories. The lower shelves were deep enough for records, and there would still be room for Megan's fairy tales, his mother's art books, his father's technical manuals. There was room here for everything, for everyone. And a desk. He'd have a desk in the window, facing the fireplace in the winter and the wide bay of windows in the summer. Like scenes in a movie Jeff saw his father seated at the desk in the yellow glow of a lamp, while he and Megan stretched out on a thick red carpet, reading in front of the fireplace, and his mother curled on a soft leather sofa. Though he'd been far more likely, until Grandfather came and disapproved, to be watching television, the vision of the family in the library caught at him like the smell of home-baked pie.

"It's this room," Jeff said aloud, shaking his head free of the images. "Or this house. It's getting to me as much as it does to Megan."

Trying to keep his mind on his business, he flashed his light once more around the empty shelves. If only they had left one book with a name inscribed on its flyleaf, he'd know who the key belonged to. But there was nothing. Reluctantly Jeff returned to the parlor, heading back to the dining room.

At the doorway to the hall he stopped. After the gloom of the library and parlor, where little or no light crept in through the wall of bushes and boarded up windows, the brightness of the front entry made him blink. Almost before he realized it, the sudden light put him on guard. His pulse began pounding in his throat. The hallway was no longer shadowed.

The light didn't come from the dining room, where the chandelier struggled beneath its coating of grime. Nor was it from the hot summer sun, passing in its southwest course. Since he and Megan had entered the house, the sun had shifted from the side to the front, beating down in the early afternoon on the blank upstairs windows and the peeling front porch, moving through midafternoon to the far west side of the house. It was not the beam of his flashlight either, nor any reflection of light from it or from the feeble rays of the chandelier. But the hallway was filled with light.

"Megan," Jeff called, in a hoarse whisper. His mouth was dry, and his throat squeezed shut around his words. "Megan, are you there?"

As he spoke, he crouched and jumped to the Oriental carpet, trying to stay below the level of the glass panels in the door. Bent down like a runner, he edged up to the doors and peered through the scalloped border that was etched on the glass. For a moment nothing odd registered. Some five feet from him was the solid dark wood of the front door. Around the door were the narrow, leaded-glass panes. Sunlight poured through them, bouncing off the worn, silvery wood of the porch. And then he realized.

"Megan," Jeff croaked again, scuttling across the carpet toward the dining room. "Megan, where are you?"

But instead of Megan's voice, the shrillness of a doorbell cut the still air. Jeff flattened himself on the carpet as the sound screamed around him. Then he elbowed himself forward onto the rough matting of the dining room floor.

"Megan," he called above the shriek of the

bell. "Megan, answer me. Where are you?"

He reached the edge of the canvas-covered table in the center of the room and ducked under it. For a moment he couldn't see, as the canvas fell behind him, cutting off the light. The bell rang on, beating against his eardrums. He sat up and cracked his head against the tabletop. He blinked. Megan was crouched opposite him on all fours, frozen by the bell, her mouth open, and her eyes black in her pale face. Seeing him she threw herself forward, pressing up close beside him. The bell stopped.

"They'll find us," she said. "I know they'll find us. What'll we do?"

"Shhh," Jeff hushed her. "Don't move."

Huddled beneath the canvas they listened, waiting for the footsteps at the front door. But none came. Silence fell around them and enveloped the house once more. Carefully Jeff raised a corner of the canvas and peeked out. There was no sign of another person.

"Come on," Jeff whispered. "We'll crawl under the table to get as close to the kitchen door as we can, and then we'll make a run for it. Maybe it was just a salesman or something at the door."

The legs of the table were attached to two pedestals, ornately carved at the base into claws. Megan crawled over them heading back where she had been. Jeff was right behind her when the bell sounded again, shivering the entire house.

"Keep your head down, and hurry," Jeff said, shoving her toward the kitchen door. The bell stopped for an instant, and as Jeff followed Megan, it blasted them yet a third time. Jeff lifted his palm. The bell stopped. He ran his hand over the floor and felt the bulge beneath the rotted matting. He pressed it, and the bell rang.

"Jeff, come on! Hurry," Megan shouted from the kitchen. "They're getting impatient."

Instead, Jeff hit the button again and stuck his head out from under the canvas. "I'd like some more soup, please," he said. Megan stared at him.

"Are you crazy? Come on."

Jeff pumped the button and the bell rang on and off. "It's another of those servant things," he said. "When you're eating dinner and it's time for the maid to take the plates, you press the button under the table with your foot, and the bell rings in the kitchen. I've seen it in old movies."

"That loud?" Megan crawled back and pushed the button.

"I don't suppose it sounds that loud when the house is full of furniture and people. But I think we should get out of here anyway."

"Why? Did you find something?"

"I'll tell you outside," Jeff said, pushing her toward the door.

"Wait, I have to say good-bye." Megan snatched the cone down from the house phone. " 'Bye, House. I want to see the chandelier lit when I come back and the unicorn all polished. And Jeff wants . . ." She turned to her brother. "What do you want from the house, Jeff?"

"Books on the shelves," Jeff answered without thinking. Then he grabbed Megan's hand. "And to get out of here now."

"Books," she called into the phone. "Jeff wants books. I have to go. 'Bye."

She dropped the phone and let Jeff drag her across the kitchen to the door. He unlocked the dead bolt, turned on his flashlight, and pulled Megan with him down the steps. As fast as he could he led them through the cluttered cellar and up the dark stairs to the exit. He pushed open the hatch slowly, half expecting to find someone waiting for them in the now shady driveway. But he saw no one when he popped up his head and half lifted Megan out of the cellar behind him. He dropped the hatch, spun the combination, and locked the cellar, leaving the numbers as he had found them.

"What's the big hurry all of a sudden?" Megan asked when they were wheeling their bikes under the arch of hedge at the front of the house. "What did you find?"

"I didn't find anything." Jeff looked back down the flagstone path. "It's the door. There was a plywood panel across it when I got here and now it's gone. Anyone could have come in the front door while we were inside."

"They could?" Megan's small hand tightened around Jeff's wrist. "Because the door was that way when I got here."

For a moment they both stared down the broken flagstone walk to the front of the house. Then Jeff said, "That means that someone removed the plywood after I came."

"And before I did," Megan said again. "But there wasn't anyone outside, and no one on the porch. I'm sure of it. Where could someone go with a plywood door?"

Jeff pointed to the side of the porch. "Not far," he said. "It's right there."

"Whoever it was didn't just take down a door and disappear."

"No, our visitor didn't disappear." Jeff swallowed twice. "Whoever it was took the door down in order to go inside."

They watched the old house. Light caught in the upstairs windows. Nothing moved, nothing changed. Yet the front door was visible now, and functional. Someone had opened it and gone inside. Someone had looked out through the border of glass panels and down the flagstone path to the arch in the hedge where Jeff and Megan now stood.

"Maybe you'd better give me the key," Jeff said. "We can leave it on the front porch or something, with a note."

Megan plunged her hand into her shorts pocket and gasped. "No, we can't."

"We don't have to know who owns the house. The owner's here."

"We can't because I don't have it." Megan looked up at him, both pockets pulled out, empty. "I left it on the kitchen table."

Eight

"You left it there?" Jeff heard his own voice, loud behind the red rush of anger that flushed his face. "How could you leave it there?"

"I'm sorry, Jeff." Because he so seldom shouted at her, Megan was startled and genuinely frightened. "I only put it down for a minute, when I climbed on the chair. I'll go back."

"You can't go back. We're lucky we got out when we did this time." Jeff straddled his bike, one foot on the ground and the other on the pedal, and looked again at the front door. "We can't ever go back."

"Never?" Megan asked, close to tears.

"Never," Jeff said, too angry to care how she felt. "You fixed it so we can never go back. Come on. Let's go home."

Deliberately he pushed off and rode at his normal pace, ignoring Megan until they stopped at a corner to cross. When he glanced back at her then, her cheeks were bright red and smeared with the tears she tried to brush away before Jeff noticed. She clamped her jaw shut to stifle the panting breaths of her effort to keep up with him.

"You go first," he said, stopping on the other side of the street to let her pass. She hesitated, slipping a still-scared look up at him, but didn't speak. "Go as slow as you want. I'll follow you. Just go on, Megan. What difference does a stupid key make?"

Riding after her down the sidewalk, he asked himself the same thing. Why should he be so angry with her for leaving the key behind, especially when it was his idea to return it to the house anyway? By now, whoever had opened the front door was probably standing in the kitchen with the key in hand, wondering where it came from — or knowing where it came from! A cold chill clamped on Jeff's neck at the thought of someone's entering the front of the house while he and Megan were creeping up from the cellar. Surely if their presence were known, the stranger in the house would have confronted them, had them arrested, or listened to their story and sent them off with a stern lecture about the sanctity of other people's property. And considering the noise they'd made, and the evidence they'd left, how could the person not know?

But if by some miracle they were undetected,

then it didn't matter. The key was back where it belonged, and he and Megan were not only safe, but also not in trouble. So what difference did it make? Not until they turned in the driveway did Jeff come up with the answer.

I can't go back, he thought, and his stomach swooped as if he'd just hit the bottom of a steep hill on his bike. I'm mad because I can't go back.

His excuse was gone. He no longer had even the flimsiest reason for doing what was desperately right for him and wrong by any other standard. Even in his mind, sneaking back into the house was trespassing, and going there to retrieve the key smacked entirely too much of stealing. To have found a haven from Grandfather's disapproval and the misery it caused at home, only to lose it again, gave a deathblow to his rising hopes for the summer.

Hidden behind the tangle of hedges, the unexplored territories of the house were now off limits. Its mysteries were beyond him. Who had draped the dining room furniture, only to abandon it to bats and spiders? Who had left the dusty flowers on the kitchen table? Who had stripped the library of its books? Jeff wanted to know almost as much as he wanted to know who had unbarred the front door, and what that stranger planned for the neglected house. Without the key, he'd never find out. Worse, without the key, he could not escape

Grandfather. He couldn't spend all day at the park, and if he stayed home, he was sure to get in trouble. And worst of all, that guaranteed that the half-heard, irritated exchanges between his parents, and their even more unsettling silences, would continue. That's what difference the key made.

"It's Jeff's turn," Mrs. Armstead was saying to Megan as he slouched into the kitchen, letting the screen door slap behind him. "You'll have all the chances you want to set the table next week."

"That's all right, Mom, I'll do it," Megan insisted.

"You'll take a bath." Turning her attention to Jeff, his mother stopped chopping green peppers for the spaghetti sauce. "Are you sure your research wasn't excavation? You're both filthy."

"You just aren't used to seeing Megan that way, Mom. I'm like this all summer."

"No doubt," she said, swooping the pepper off the cutting board into the hot olive oil. "But that's no excuse. Go wash your hands and set the table. Megan should be done in time for you to take a shower before dinner."

"He can go ahead. I'll do it." Megan looked at her hands and rubbed them hard on her shorts. "I'm not really dirty."

"It's all an illusion, is it?" Mrs. Armstead paused in her flurry of cooking. Her face relaxed as she looked at the children. She bent and kissed Megan on the tip of the nose. "See what kind of a ring illusion leaves in the bathtub," she said. "Off with you."

Megan sighed and dragged herself out of the kitchen. A few minutes later they heard the water running and the fan, but without the usual accompaniment of Megan's tub songs.

"You want to tell me what happened?"

"With what?"

"Not what, who," Jeff's mother answered. "There's something up when your sister volunteers to do your chores for you."

"I'm just tired of her tagging along." Jeff dried his hands on a paper towel and opened the refrigerator. "Isn't there anything to eat around here?"

"All this family thinks about is food!" Mrs. Armstead slammed the chopping board down on the counter. Jeff jumped. "Your grandfather wants bananas on his cereal, not peaches, and half and half, not whole milk. I cannot go to the grocery store every day. I will not go to the grocery store every day. If you're hungry, wait until dinner."

Jeff took a couple of carrot sticks from the jar on the shelf and closed the refrigerator gently. "I'll go if you need something."

"I don't need anything except some peace and quiet." She sliced onions in silence, then dabbed at her eyes with the sleeve of her shirt.

"You want to go read the paper? I can do that."

"It's all right, Jeff. It's just the onions," she said, dumping them and the minced garlic into the pot. "Now what's this about Megan?"

"Nothing, Mom, forget it."

"I won't forget it. Did she try to help you with your research?"

"Tried is right." Jeff snapped the end off a crisp carrot stick. "Tried and failed. And then she expects me not to get mad when she messes things up."

"You can certainly understand how she feels." She added tomato paste to the pot, a spoonful of sugar and some spices, and then stood back, stirring the sauce. "It isn't easy being a younger sister."

"What about being an older brother?" Jeff crunched another carrot. "Don't worry. It doesn't matter."

"But she wants to make it up to you."

"I told her not to try."

"Good. Don't make it an excuse to refuse to have her around." Mrs. Armstead looked into the pot, added water, and lowered the heat before she clapped on the lid. "Things are difficult enough without adding that to the mix. Let's set the table."

Jeff yanked open the silverware drawer. "I guess we can't wait for Dad."

His mother stopped and looked at him. "In fact, I think tonight we should wait for your father." She watched Jeff take out five forks and spoons and knives and lay them around the table. "I'm sorry I snapped at you," she said. "Tell me about this project of yours. Is there anything I can help with?"

"It's too late now." He lifted five plates out of the cupboard.

"Why too late?" She was folding napkins in triangles and smoothing them beside the forks.

"I just can't do it now, that's all." Through the window Jeff could see the tomato patch where he'd found the key. "I was wondering about an old house we saw."

"There are quite a few in town. Arborton was founded in 1869, after all." She was talking casually, with only half her attention, listening for what was really bothering him. Now her face brightened. "Why don't you ask Grandfather? He could tell you about old houses, including his own property. That's a wonderful idea."

"I don't know, Mom."

"It's perfect." Her enthusiasm built. "He'd be busy, out of the house. He needs to get out in the world more. He'd be so pleased if you asked him."

"Would he?"

"Of course he would. It's a wonderful opportunity — "

"To get to know him," Jeff finished for her. "I tried that with the tomatoes, remember?"

"Forget the tomatoes." His mother began slicing cucumber for salad. "There's so much he could tell you. Grandfather lived here when the town was just a village, and your grandmother came from one of the founding families."

"What's this about forgetting the tomatoes?" Grandfather's disembodied voice interrupted her, filling the room. Mrs. Armstead turned to look down the front hallway, and Jeff swung around toward the dining room. But Grandfather was outside, standing at the kitchen window.

"There's weeding to be done in the garden," he said. "Jeffrey should take care of that tomorrow."

"I'm sure he'd be happy to, Dad." Jeff's mother squinted at him through the screen. Jeff snitched a chunk of cucumber while her back was turned, popping it into his mouth.

"Let him speak for himself, Liz. The boy's not dumb."

But with the cucumber jamming his tongue, Jeff was momentarily silenced. He could only nod vigorously.

"What's that?" Grandfather asked.

Jeff's Adam's apple bounced up and down

as he tried to swallow the cucumber whole so that he could speak.

"Answer me, boy. You have a problem with that?"

Jeff shook his head, still swallowing, stretching his neck until the cucumber dropped like a dead weight to his stomach, leaving a small circle of pain at the base of his throat. "No, sir," he wheezed, finally. "I can do it tomorrow."

"That's better. Speak up when you're spoken to."

"Jeff's got a wonderful idea, Dad," Mrs. Armstead told him when he came inside. "How would you like to show him around the village this summer, teach him some local history? There's so much you could tell him."

"Town's not the same as it was in my day."

"It's not really so different. Lots of the original houses are still standing. Some have even been restored. You could show Jeff how it used to be. He'd learn some family history, too."

"There's nothing to tell." Grandfather frowned. "The boy's not interested in old houses."

"The ones with turrets and attics are kind of neat," Jeff volunteered.

"It takes work to keep them up," Grandfather said. "These days people don't want the headaches of an old house."

"It's the old plumbing they don't want," Mrs.

Armstead said. "The houses are lovely, with all that space."

"What about the ghosts, Mom? Would you be afraid of them?"

"You know there are no such things, Jeff."

"I'm not so sure," Grandfather surprised them by saying. The old man spread his gnarled fingers and looked down at his hands as if they belonged to someone else. The light winked off his glasses. "Old houses keep their ghosts, I think, until new ones move in."

"Don't be giving Jeff ideas. What you mean is that they have a past, and memories." Mrs. Armstead set the salad bowl on the table and started to turn away. Her glance swung past Grandfather, then back to him. She paused, and touched his arm. "You look tired, Dad. Are you feeling all right? Maybe you should lie down before dinner."

Immediately Grandfather straightened up, squaring his shoulders and lifting his chin. "It's all this talk about old things. Better to let the past die, I say. Dinner almost ready?"

"I thought we'd wait for Gene tonight." She spoke rapidly, before he could object. "The children miss having meals with him. I thought you wouldn't mind. You do understand."

Grandfather stood up. "No sense wasting the light. Come along, Jeffrey. A crash course in gardening now might avoid disaster tomorrow."

That night Jeff lay in the heavy summer dark of his half of the room, his hands behind his head, staring up at the invisible ceiling. Grandfather had gone out, and his parents sat in wary silence behind their books in the living room. On the other side of the partition he could hear Megan's soft rustlings as she wriggled from one position to another. He tried to blot out her small sounds by concentrating on the chorus of cicadas as he conjured up a meeting with the owner of the house on Grove Street.

He would give himself up as the trespasser who had returned the key, and offer to work in penance for his crime. Surely no one could object if he trimmed the bushes and cut the grass, and pruned the roses to bloom on the arbor trellis. At least he would be there, on the premises. His fingers itched to replace the sundial on its base, open again to the sun. Perhaps if he worked hard enough, the owner would invite him in and let him help restock the library shelves. His eyes closed, and he felt the silky texture of the polished wood beneath his fingertips. He could almost smell the leather-bound books, all stamped in gold, that the owner would at last trust him to unpack.

"Jeff?" Megan's whisper stirred his half

dream. "Jeff, are you still awake?"

"No." He squeezed his eyes shut, imagining the friendship that would grow between him and the unknown owner. Perhaps he'd have a son who would invite Jeff to spend weekends with him. "Come anytime, Jeff," the owner would say. "This house is as much yours as ours. Make yourself at home, Jeff. . . ."

"Jeff? You are awake."

"I wasn't, but I am now." Jeff rolled over. "What's the matter?"

"I'm sorry."

"I know. Just forget it, will you?" It sounded harsher than he meant it. He flopped onto his back. "It doesn't really matter, Megan. Honest. I was going to put the key back, anyway. You just saved me the trouble."

"But now you'll never get a reward."

"People don't give rewards for old keys. That was a stupid idea."

"The house liked us. It's going to miss us."

"The house is not alive. It can't miss anybody."

"And we can't go back, not even to visit?"

"No." Saying it out loud to Megan made it painfully true for Jeff. The house still haunted him, with its forlorn eyes and empty spaces. How could he not go back? "Forget it, Megan. Go to sleep."

"We'd have to go back, though, if we still had

the key." Her small voice came through the thickening dark of night and sleep.

"I suppose so," Jeff mumbled, rolling over on his side. "But we don't. Good night, Megan."

Nine

Weeds wouldn't dare grow in Grandfather's tomato patch, not yet, Jeff thought two days later as he again stood in front of the clean square of dirt. But he dropped carefully down on his hands and knees among the hairy green plants and began his now daily chore of loosening the soil with the hand cultivator as Grandfather had shown him. Before he moved even an inch, he checked in all four directions. If he damaged just one of the plants, he'd never hear the end of it.

It hardly seemed necessary to trim the edges of the plot, or to inspect each plant for tomato worms and other pests. But Grandfather didn't believe in pesticides or messy gardens. He said it was better to weed for fifteen minutes every day than to labor for an hour once a week. And Jeff was determined to avoid Grandfather's criticism, especially since he'd left Jeff alone and unsupervised and gone off again on his town business. As Jeff moved cautiously on to the next row, Mrs. Armstead came out and looked around the yard.

"Is Megan out here with you?"

He shook his head. "I haven't seen her all morning. She was up before I was."

"She was up at dawn yesterday, too, and Grandfather sent her back to bed. You didn't see her at all?" His mother sounded alarmed. It was not unusual for Megan to wake early, but she rarely woke alone. Megan liked company in the morning. "She didn't talk to you?"

"Her bed was made. I thought she was with you."

"She's been awfully quiet since you two had your quarrel. Surely she didn't go out by herself, to the park or something." Real anxiety edged Mrs. Armstead's voice. "But her bike's gone."

"She's around somewhere." Jeff tried to cover his own concern beneath the superior tone of the older brother. The idea that gripped him stirred fear for Megan as well as a tingle of excitement at the base of his rib cage. He stood up slowly, his knees caked with brown dirt. "I suppose you want me to go look for her."

"Somebody has to, and I'd better stay here." His mother glanced around the yard again. "This isn't like Megan. I'll check next door. I can't imagine where she's gotten to."

But Jeff could. He knew as surely as if she'd announced it, which in a way she had. He knew where to look as certainly as he felt the dirt crumbling off his skin and the wooden handle of the cultivator slipping out of his muddy palm. Knowing made his throat tight and his lungs short of breath.

"Don't worry, Mom," he managed to say. "She didn't go far."

"Wherever she went is already too far," his mother said in a deliberately calm voice. "Go now. Grandfather's chore can wait."

"I'll get my bike."

Jeff tore down Grove Street at full speed, hoping to see Megan's orange flag waving ahead of him. He rode directly to the house. He skidded under the arch of the overgrown hedge and bumped across the rough lawn to the driveway. Tucked back beneath the honeysuckle he saw it, the small red bicycle with its brave orange flag.

"She couldn't get in," he told himself, dropping his bike and running back to the cellar door. "How would she open the lock?"

But the lock was open, the hatch turned back on the mound of tall grass. Without pausing Jeff ran down the steps into the dark cellar. Blindly he stumbled through the clutter, hurrying despite the cracks to his shins and elbows. Because of him, Megan was alone somewhere in the old house, and he had to find her before anyone else did. He reached the kitchen steps at last and charged up them two at a time, praying that Megan had not locked herself in with the dead bolt. He threw himself at the door and burst into the kitchen.

He knew at once it was empty. Jeff leaned against the door, panting, listening to the hollow, unoccupied sounds of the kitchen. He heard the rasp of his own breathing, the scrape of his shoes on the floor, the rustle of his shirt when he closed the door behind him. Then he pushed off across the room, vaguely aware that it had changed, but too intent on Megan to question how. Catching his breath he was aware that the air was fresher and cooler. But he went on, through the door to the dining room.

It was gone. At first sight it appeared that the room they entered two days earlier had been stripped from the house and replaced by a fantasy. The windows, though still shuttered on the outside, would have been no competition for the chandelier that glittered above Jeff's head, not even on the brightest of white winter days. Each crystal twinkled and sparkled in the light of two dozen tiny bulbs, casting a sunburst of light upward onto the plaster garlands, and throwing its own reflection down to the swept and shining floor. The furniture was uncovered, the huge pieces reclaiming their places in the room with polished dignity. A scent of lemon tinged the air, and cut the sweetness of a bowl of peonies set at the center of the table.

Wherever Jeff looked there were changes. The rotted drapes were gone from the window, replaced by simple swags of lace. On the chest beneath the window was a silver tea set, and at each end of the long table, flanking the crystal flower bowl, was a silver candelabrum. Freed of its enchantment of dust, the deep mahogany of the wood gleamed richly red. Even the walls had come alive, their naked scars now shielded by paintings. A still life of tumbled fruit added color above the buffet, and a series of delicate drawings balanced it on the opposite wall. Only at the head of the table was the wall still blank, marked with the outline of a large oval frame. All this Jeff took in as he stood there, barely drawing breath. But as startling as these details were, it was the sight at the foot of the table that raised the hair on his neck.

Two places were set there, on linen mats with heavy glass tumblers and pretty pottery plates. Between them was a covered platter of sandwiches, peanut-butter-and-jelly sandwiches, just as Megan had ordered. And next to that was a bowl of fruit and another covered plate heaped high with chocolate chip cookies.

At each plate there was a silver napkin ring,

engraved. Half afraid to look, Jeff tiptoed up to the table. His eyes followed the intertwined letters of elegant script. Unbelieving, he reached out and with the tip of his finger traced the letters — *MSA* and *JCA.* Megan Suzanne and Jeffrey Charles Armstead.

He snatched his finger back. Dozens of names could match those initials, and dozens of people ate peanut butter and jelly for lunch. The house was not providing Megan's lunch to order. That was impossible. There was no such thing as a house with ears or the magic to fulfill wishes. He must not waste time on weird coincidences. He had to find Megan. Still, as he left the room, Jeff had the eerie sense that he'd rejected a gift.

At the hallway he paused long enough to make sure that no one was on the front porch or opening the front door. He glanced once down the corridor to the stairs that rose to the upper stories of the house. Seeing nothing, he ducked across the hall.

Whatever magic altered the dining room did not extend to the parlor. It was still dark and bare. Outside branches tapped like fingernails on the broken wooden shutters and picked at the shadows in the dim room. There was no sign of Megan and no obvious place for her to be hiding. On tiptoe Jeff crossed to the library door. It was open a crack, the key in its lock, but Jeff could see nothing more than the rows of empty shelves on the far side of the room. He thought he heard a dry, flaky rustle near the door and held his breath to listen. When it wasn't repeated, he gripped the knob and swung the door back. Triangular slices of the room appeared as the door opened on silent hinges. Jeff thought it, too, was empty, like the parlor, until he saw the overstuffed chair in front of the fireplace. It was a dark red leather, shiny enough to reflect the firelight, and set at an angle to catch the maximum of heat. Neatly stacked on the dusty grate were three small logs on a nest of kindling, ready for the first fall match.

"There you are. What took you so long?"

"Megan!" Jeff jerked backward, thumping into the door. "What do you think you're doing?"

She peered at him from around the winged corner of the chair. "I'm reading."

"Mom's worried half to death and you're reading?" Jeff stepped in front of the chair. "You barely know how."

"I can too read." Megan sat cross-legged, surrounded by the chair, hardly making a dent in the soft leather of its cushions. A fat book covered her lap, open at a full-page illustration of *Sleeping Beauty*.

"You asked for books," she said, and pointed to the shelves beneath the glass-fronted ones. "I thought we ought to read them."

"We shouldn't even be here," Jeff hissed, trying to keep his voice at something like a whisper in spite of the scare she'd given him. "And you're sitting here reading as if you own the place. Where did you get this?"

"Right there, I told you. On the shelf."

Jeff swung around. Under his shelves, where he imagined displaying his models, were two rows of brightly bound books. The one in Megan's lap matched a set of fairy tales from different countries. The other series was a sort of science encyclopedia. At the end of the row was a small white card. *More to come*, it read.

"Megan, we have to get out of here." Jeff took the book in one hand and pulled Megan out of the chair with the other.

"I don't want to go home. I like it here. We can't go before lunch. It's all ready. I was just waiting for you."

"That isn't ours. It can't be. We don't belong here." Jeff jammed the book back on the shelf and started to drag Megan to the door. "I told you we couldn't come back."

"But the house wants us." She fumbled in her pocket. "And I got the key. Now we can come back whenever we want."

Jeff stopped in the doorway and faced her. "Somebody else lives here, Megan. Can't you understand that? It isn't our house. Another family is moving in. Why would this stuff be here otherwise?"

"Because I asked for it. You heard me."

"That's some kind of an accident. You can't just make yourself at home in somebody else's house."

"How do you know it is somebody else's?" Megan planted herself in the doorway, unwilling to follow him. "You found the key. The house let us in."

"Listen to me, Megan. People pick out houses to live in. Houses do not pick out people." He put a hand to his forehead and addressed the ceiling, rolling his eyes. "This is crazy. Listen to me. I can't believe I'm arguing with you about this."

"What about the lunch, if you're so smart?"

"It's for the people who live here, can't you see?"

"Then where are they? I don't see them."

"Maybe they're out shopping. I don't know. But we aren't the only ones who eat peanut butter and jelly or chocolate chip cookies. Name me someone who doesn't."

"Paulette Donnelly. She's allergic."

"Forget it. Believe whatever you want, but come on. Mom's got the whole neighborhood looking for you."

"Suppose I prove it to you." She came after him into the parlor. "Would you believe the house wanted us if I could prove it?"

"You can't, so what's the point? There's no such thing as a magic house." Jeff pushed her behind him while he checked the front door and hallway. "Keep your voice down, will you? We don't want to get caught now."

"We aren't doing anything wrong," Megan insisted. "Did you see the chandelier? It's just the way I wanted, and the unicorn, too."

But Jeff didn't stop. He tugged her through the dining room to the kitchen door.

"The house did what I asked, Jeff, see?" She pulled away from him to look again at the room. "Except that it didn't hang all the pictures. I want to know what goes there," she said, pointing to the dark oval stain on the wall.

"You won't find out, unless you sell the new owners some Girl Scout cookies. The paintings are for them, not us."

"But I can prove it." Megan swung around, her hands on her hips, her small jaw set. "Promise me you'll come back one more time."

"We can't come back." Yet a part of him knew he couldn't stay away. More than anything Jeff wanted to feel the weight of the key in his pocket, and with it the right to unlock the doors of the old house. Jeff wanted to believe as Megan did, that the house was theirs and that the shelves in the library were his to fill, that he could claim a seat in that soft golden light. "How could you prove it?" he asked.

"You have to tell me what you want." Megan slipped past him into the kitchen. She lifted the speaking tube from its hook on the wall and blew into it. "And I'll order it."

"What I want you can't order. Magic can't buy this house for us. Let's get out of here before someone finds us."

"Make a real wish, Jeff. You have to ask for something, something you really want or it won't work. Like this." Megan closed her eyes tight, bunching her face in concentration. "House, this is very important. I wouldn't ask except for Jeff. I have to make him believe."

"Megan, you're crazy," Jeff whispered, caught up in her conviction that the house could hear them.

"I want one of the turret rooms with a big old bed and a dollhouse all my own," Megan said, ignoring him. "Then I can come and visit whenever I want."

"No, you can't," Jeff said. "You can't ask for a room of your own in a house that doesn't belong to you."

She opened her eyes. "Why not?"

"Because it can't happen, that's why not."

"But if it does, you'll admit I'm right."

"It isn't going to happen." Jeff fell back against the kitchen counter in exasperation. "Then you'll have to admit I'm right."

Megan's eyes snapped shut again. "A real dollhouse," she said into the speaking tube. "It has to be wood, not plastic, with stairs and window eyes like yours. I know it's a lot to ask, and I wouldn't, but it's the only way to convince Jeff. And could you please put up the other painting in the dining room?"

"Did you bring in those flowers?" Jeff suddenly noticed the vase on the table. Slowly the difference in the kitchen dawned on him. The dried bouquet was gone, fresh blossoms in its place. The shutters of the upper half of the window were folded back, and light poured into the room.

"They were already here," Megan said, looking pleased with herself, as if she'd already proved her point. "And the window was open."

Jeff felt it, too, the sluffing off of decay. The house seemed to be awakening. It threw back its shutters to let in the light, and shook the dust from its crystal chandelier. Everywhere he looked Jeff saw evidence of its new life. Perhaps the key he found unlocked not a door, but a spell of abandonment cast upon it. He could almost believe it, standing there in the fresh sweep of air, until he saw the shining kettle on the stove and the washed mug draining in the sink.

"Let's go," he said to his sister, hanging up the speaking tube. "Mom's going to think we're both lost."

This time Megan followed him without argument. It wasn't until they were outside the hedge, riding home on their bikes that Jeff remembered to ask her how she got in.

"I can remember numbers just as well as you can," she said. "I just turned the combination."

"And the note on the books?" Jeff asked. "I suppose the house left that for you."

"It did." Her dark head bobbed up and down in agreement. "You asked for books, and you got books."

"Were there names in any of them? Did you look at the front to see whose books they were?"

Her bike wobbled as she looked up at him. "They're mine, of course. The fairy-tale book has my name in it, Megan S."

Ten

"I didn't just quit, if that's what you think." Jeff sank the cultivator deep into the clotted soil at Grandfather's feet. "I had to go find Megan."

"So your mother said."

"I'm supposed to be at the park." Jeff chopped again at the ground. It was all right for the tomatoes to wait on Megan, but they couldn't be put off for batting practice. "I'm missing Little League."

"Chores come first." Grandfather stood at the edge of the garden. Crouched at his feet, Jeff could see the faded blue cuffs of his overalls and the mud-streaked toes of his work shoes. His shadow fell across Jeff's shoulders, but the stripe of shade did not cool Jeff's temper any.

"I'd have been back in an hour," he muttered. Anyone else would have let him go, anyone but Grandfather. He dug angrily at the roots.

"Do it right," Grandfather said.

Jeff made himself work the soil more gently, wishing the old man away. But the two feet remained planted in the grass, set apart like a soldier's at parade rest.

"You found Megan, then." Grandfather made it sound more like a statement than a question, but Jeff nodded anyway. "Don't you children know better than to go off without telling anyone?"

Jeff sighed and sat back on his heels. Even when he didn't do anything wrong, he got the lecture.

"We're supposed to leave a note, but Megan's writing isn't so good yet," he said, trying to explain. "And it isn't as if she knew where she was going," he added in a conscious stretching of the truth. But after all, if she had really understood what she was getting into, even Megan wouldn't have gone back to the old house. "She was just riding her bike around."

"And you happened to see her? You didn't know where she was?"

Jeff pulled a piece of clover from the border. "She didn't tell me, if that's what you mean."

"It's not what I mean." Grandfather bit the words off sharply, like the snapping of pruning shears. Jeff kept his head down, concentrating on the green stems and flowers at his fingertips. Afraid to look up, he waited for the rumble of Grandfather's voice to become a growl. Instead, Grandfather bent down, so close that Jeff heard the cracking of his joints, and picked a clover.

"Four leaves brings luck." He held it out to Jeff. "Want it?"

"I guess so, sure." Jeff brushed off his hands and glanced around for some place to put it. With four-leaf clovers, you needed luck just to keep them whole. He settled for cupping it in his palm.

"What I meant was that you mustn't let your sister wander away on her own." Grandfather remained hunkered down beside Jeff, his gnarled hands hanging between his knees. At that range his harsh voice sounded almost conversational, even friendly. "Discourage her."

Jeff snorted, and the clover fluttered. "Have you ever tried to discourage Megan when she wants to do something?"

The corners of Grandfather's mouth moved, but he didn't smile. He only nodded, and his shoulder brushed briefly against Jeff's. "She's got a lot of spunk, that girl, I will say, and imagination. But we can't let it get out of hand."

"Tell that to Mom and Dad."

"I'm telling you." Again his words snapped a command. "Watch out for her."

"I'm not her baby-sitter." Jeff wanted no further responsibility for Megan's behavior, order or no order.

"But you are her brother." Grandfather stood up. "That should be enough."

"I don't ask her to follow me around," Jeff protested, waving his hands. The clover blew off his palm, and he scrambled after it. "That's the whole trouble. She has to go wherever I go."

"Then you'll have to think twice about where that is."

"But that's not fair. Suppose I want to be by myself?" Still on his hands and knees, Jeff looked up. "I sure can't do that around here."

"No, you can't, can you." Grandfather bent and retrieved the clover. He spun it in a green whirl between his thumb and forefinger. "Sharing your room because of me makes it difficult."

"I didn't mean that exactly." Jeff flushed and ducked his head, stroking the green bed of clover again as if he were searching for another lucky piece.

"Of course you did. Say what you mean, mean what you say." Grandfather made it another command, as if he expected Jeff to salute in response. "Everyone needs privacy."

"Except Megan," Jeff said. "She likes it this way."

"But you could do without the company."

"I don't have any room, that's all. There's no room for my stuff."

Again Grandfather nodded. "So that explains your sudden interest in the historical homes of Arborton. You think you'd like one of those old ruins as long as it had a large and preferably spooky attic where you could be alone."

"In a place like that it wouldn't matter how many people visited," Jeff said, thinking of the golden quiet of his library. "It wouldn't have to have an attic, even."

"As long as it had space, so you could be out of the reach of visiting relatives, I suppose."

"Exactly," Jeff said, bobbing his head up and down before he realized what he'd said. "I mean, no. That is, I don't mind your visiting."

"Just my staying," Grandfather said.

"No, really," Jeff stuttered, looking up. His ears burned with embarrassment. There was no point in denying the truth, but he tried. "That's not what I meant."

Grandfather didn't respond. He handed Jeff the clover and pointed to the base of one of the squatty tomato plants. "That one needs a little more work," he said, and turned slowly away toward the house.

In spite of the clover, Jeff's day did not improve. He was too late even to shag balls with the coach after practice, and when he got home, Mrs. Armstead sent him to play with

Megan, who was confined to the house and yard for the rest of the week.

"Go fish," Jeff said.

"But you have nines. I know you have nines." Megan struggled to hold her cards in fan shape in both hands. Jeff shook his head.

"Fish," he said again.

"Mom said not to cheat."

"I'm not cheating." Jeff snapped his cards into a pack. "I don't have nines. Can't you tell the difference yet between sixes and nines?"

He was sorry immediately. Megan rarely misread numbers or letters anymore and was humiliated when she did. But Jeff felt cheated not out of a mere game, but out of a day, perhaps an entire summer. Because Megan was grounded, he had to stay home. Because she'd gone back to the house, he'd missed baseball practice. It was easy to ignore his part in her punishment and feel sorry for himself, but it didn't change anything.

"A nine does look like an upside down six," he said in apology. "Go on, fish."

Carefully she folded the fan of cards and set it beside her on the porch. Jeff watched her rummage through the pile of cards between them before choosing one.

"Your turn," she said, shuffling through her deck. Jeff waited until she had her hand in order.

"Sixes," he asked. "Do you have any sixes?"

"Go fish." Megan wriggled and grinned at him. He pulled a card from the pile and stared at it.

"You read it wrong," he said. Megan shook her head.

"No, it was a nine. I'm sure."

"Not the cards, the book," Jeff said. "You must have read it wrong. It couldn't have been your name."

"I can read my own name."

Jeff threw his cards down. "In print, but what about script?"

"There were a lot of squiggles and curlicues," Megan admitted. "It was written inside a sort of picture that was pasted in the book."

"A bookplate that's called, to tell who owns the book."

"I do. I own it. Megan S."

"And you're sure that's what it said?"

"Pretty sure," she said. "Aren't you going to fish?"

"No, let's not play anymore. You win." Jeff pushed his cards into the pile and began to gather up the deck. "Is that where you found the key, in the library?"

Megan shook her head. "It was right where I left it, on the table in the kitchen, next to the flowers. That's when I knew the house liked us, when I saw the flowers."

"So you decided to stay and make yourself at home."

"Lunch was all ready for us," Megan said. "I was just waiting for you."

Jeff didn't even try to talk sense to her. "But you didn't see anybody or hear anybody else?"

"Why would anybody else be in our house?"

"Never mind. Just answer me. You didn't see anybody, and you took the key. Where is it?"

Megan probed the pocket of her shorts and glanced around the porch before she pulled the key out. She handed it to Jeff.

"Now, listen," he said, closing his fist around the solid metal, warm in his palm. "You have to promise that you won't go back there, not unless you talk to me first."

"But you said — " Megan began.

"All right, all right, I know what I said. But you have to promise that you won't go alone."

She hesitated.

"Do you want both of us to spend the whole summer here on the porch? If Mom catches us, in the mood she's been in, we're really in trouble."

"Okay, I promise."

They both looked up at the sound of a car in the driveway. Backing expertly up to the porch, Mr. Armstead leaned out the window.

"Get your mother," he said, grinning. "And go pack the fishing gear. You've got one hour to get ready to go to the lake."

"Me, too?" Megan asked. "Mom says I have to stay here all week."

"Of course, you, too," her father said. "The whole family's going."

Megan leaped over the porch steps to hug her father, then tore off down the driveway to the kitchen door. "Mom! Mom!" she shouted. "Daddy says I don't have to stay home!"

"What's all that about?" Mr. Armstead asked.

"Megan's grounded," Jeff told him as she disappeared into the house.

"Megan?" Mr. Armstead raised his eyebrows. "I guess it's been an interesting day for everyone."

"How come you're home so early?" Jeff asked, not eager to field questions about Megan's adventure.

"I thought you'd never ask." Jeff's father held out his hand. "Be the first to shake the hand of the new regional manager. Come on, let's tell your mother."

"That's wonderful, Gene," she said, laughing as he waltzed her in her jeans around the kitchen. "But the lake, now? I've got a refrigerator full of food."

"It's now or never, Liz. The next two months are going to be too busy for me to get away."

"Don't worry about the refrigerator. I can

take care of it," Grandfather said from the doorway. "It's time I did some cooking for myself."

"Dad, you heard the news? I got the promotion. But they want me to take a week off now, before I start. Forget the refrigerator. Get your fishing hat."

Grandfather had changed out of his overalls for dinner. He wore a light cotton cardigan over his shirt, and a tie, and pressed khaki trousers. His broad shoulders stooped forward a little, and he gripped the doorjamb with one hand, as if for balance. He had to look up a little to his son, stretching the loose flesh of his neck.

"I think not, Gene. You young people go. You'll have a better time without me."

"Don't be silly, Dad," Jeff's mother said, too quickly. "Of course you'll come with us. How long is it since you've been there?"

"Too long to go back now," Grandfather said. "Besides, there's not enough room. You'll have quite enough stuff in the car without me."

"You can have my place, Grandfather." Megan danced over to him and took his free hand in both of hers. "Then I can sit on your lap. You have to come."

He dropped his head to look down at her as she leaned back, tugging on his hand. Even Jeff saw the softening of the lines in his face. Not a smile exactly, but a warming of expression that moved up and caught in the twinkle of his eyes.

"Young lady, did you ever think that I have better things to do than to be your car seat?"

Megan giggled, and they all laughed. She succeeded in dragging Grandfather to a chair at the table and leaned comfortably against him while Mr. and Mrs. Armstead tried to change his mind.

"It's only for a week, Dad. We can try to catch that big bass you used to tell me about."

But Grandfather shook his head. "That was in another time. I haven't fished that lake since . . . since before you were born. I wouldn't know where to start. No, I'll stay here. A little peace and quiet for a change can't hurt."

"You don't know where I keep anything," Mrs. Armstead said. "How will you find what you need?"

"I've managed to find everything I need for the past forty years, Liz. I guess I can handle another week. It'll be good for us all."

He looked directly at Jeff, his eyes gleaming like blue fire behind his glasses. It was a challenge, and Jeff knew he had to meet it, uncertain as he was about its terms. He hesitated, but only for a moment.

"If you won't come with us, maybe you'd like one of us to stay here, just to keep you company."

"Are you volunteering?" The blue eyes

pinned him where he stood. Jeff shrugged.

"Sure, if you say so." He met Grandfather's eyes without flinching.

"Never volunteer," Grandfather said. "It's one of the first things I learned in the army, when I was just a boy in what was left of Europe after the war. You go along with your father. That bass liked surface lures, as I recall. See if you have better luck than I did."

He didn't. Only when they trolled the lake — his father paddling the canoe against the wind, Jeff paddling back — did they get a hit, a bony northern pike. Even when Jeff placed the bright green Hula Popper at exactly the right spot above the bass hole, the Big One was not enticed. Glimpsed like shadows, the bass hung in the cool, deep water of the rocky shore, in the shade of the overhanging locust trees.

Above the fish, in the canoe, Jeff and his father cast their lures on the smooth green surface and reeled them in again. They listened to the scolding of a blue jay and the chatter of the red squirrels in the treetops, changed their lures, and cast again. All week during the long companionable silences, Jeff thought about Grandfather, alone at home, and wondered about the empty house on Grove Street. And all week, as he gazed into the soft, rippled surface of the lake, Jeff dreamed of the hidden house he saw flickering just beyond reach, its topaz windows gleaming out of the green depths, its doors swinging open, unlocked by shadowy keys.

Eleven

"We're home!" After being pent up in the backseat for the long drive back to Arborton, Megan burst out of the car like a cork from a bottle. She ran across the lawn and up the front steps of the unlighted house. Mrs. Armstead moved more slowly. She stepped out on the gravel driveway and shivered in spite of the warmth of the evening.

"It looks deserted," she said.

"Not for long," Jeff's father said, watching Megan. He slung a duffel bag from the trunk over his shoulder. "At least one of us is glad to be home."

"It isn't that." Mrs. Armstead reached out for his hand. "This was a wonderful week. A few more days would have been even more wonderful. One plus wonderful."

"Two-derful? I'm not sure I could handle that."

She laughed, a light note in the dusk, and squared her shoulders. "I feel as if we can handle anything now. Coming, Jeff?"

He trailed behind them as hand in hand they followed Megan to the front door. How long would the easy give-and-take and laughter between his parents last once he and Grandfather were under the same roof again?

"Grandfather, we're home!" Megan burst into the living room. "Did you miss us? Jeff caught a northern, and we had him for supper."

"The fish, not Jeff," Mr. Armstead said, setting the bag down in the hallway. "How are you, Dad? Is everything okay?"

Grandfather blinked and reached for his glasses. "You're back early. I didn't expect you until after dark."

"It's well past that now. Look outside."

"There's still some light. Days are longer in summer." But Grandfather switched on a lamp. The heavy shadows fell away, chased into the dark of porch and lawn. Squinting against the light and the nakedness of his face, Grandfather put on his glasses and swung his feet off the hassock. "I'll give you a hand with your bags."

"Jeff can take them," his mother said. "You stay put and rest. Have you had supper?"

"Now, don't start fussing at me, Liz. I don't become frail and feeble-minded just because you people walk in the door." He grabbed one end of the duffel bag and began to drag it toward the steps.

"I'll help, Grandfather. We can do it together." Megan seized the other end of the bag. Panting and straining, she pulled it across the hall after Grandfather. Jeff glanced at his parents, but Mr. Armstead held up his hand and shook his head. The three of them stood together in silence until the duffel bag was out of sight and audibly bumping its way along the upstairs hall.

"He looks awfully tired, Gene. I'll bet he hasn't had a decent meal since we left."

"I wish it were as simple as that." Mr. Armstead remained at the foot of the stairs, frowning. "We should never have left him alone here. I should have insisted he come with us."

"But you did, and he refused." Mrs. Armstead lowered her voice. "And we needed this week, Gene, to get things sorted out."

"It's what he may have sorted out that bothers me." His eyes flicked over Jeff and away again. "He knew what a disturbance it was for us to have him here. He wasn't sitting in that chair in the dark brooding over food."

"It wasn't dark, not quite," Jeff said. "The streetlights weren't on. You always say to come home when the streetlights come on."

"It was dark enough." But Jeff's father managed to smile at him. "Night does come slower in summer, doesn't it? It sneaks up on you so gradually that you don't realize the light's gone."

"You don't mean that he'd leave?" Jeff's mother asked. "In spite of everything, I don't want that. He'll have a home here as long as he needs it."

"He may not be convinced, but thanks for saying it." Mr. Armstead slipped an arm around her shoulders. "We'll just have to try harder, all of us."

"If only we had a bigger house," Mrs. Armstead said.

"Or a smaller grandfather," Jeff suggested, smiling so they would know it was a joke. They seemed not to hear.

"Where would he go?"

"I don't know," Mr. Armstead answered her. "I don't like the idea of his living alone. I'm worried about him."

"You think he's sick?" Jeff asked. A cold shiver rippled his skin. Though he considered Grandfather old, it hadn't occurred to Jeff that something might be wrong with him. His hands were stiff but strong, and if his joints creaked, he still moved with authority.

"Not sick, exactly," his father said. "Coming here may have been too much for him, too many memories after all those years."

"But it isn't as though he hasn't been back before, Gene."

"Those were all short visits. This time he's stayed, and he's been digging up the past."

"Sorting through the things he's had in storage all these years, you mean?" Mrs. Armstead nodded. "Just selling the house would be a shock, though he claims he wants nothing to do with it. I hadn't really thought about it."

"The lake, too," Jeff's father said. "You know, he proposed to my mother there, and yet he won't go back. He took her out in the canoe for a midnight paddle in the moonlight."

"Grandfather did that? Who said?"

"Too romantic for you? But that is in fact what he did." Mr. Armstead reached out to ruffle Jeff's hair. "Don't look so dismayed. Aunt Dorf told me. She was trying to explain why my father wouldn't take me fishing. All those bass feeding in the twilight, a full moon rising, and he wouldn't go. I really wanted to catch that Big One."

Jeff's mother murmured something, and pressed her cheek against his father's shoulder. Mr. Armstead tightened his arm around her, and abruptly pulled Jeff closer, tilting him to one side in a half hug.

"Don't blame Grandfather. You probably wouldn't have got it anyway," Jeff said, embarrassed by the sudden silence and the physical closeness. His parents both laughed, and

Jeff broke away. "I mean, nobody's caught that fish yet, right?"

"Just wait until next year," his father said. "I'll get it then. Meantime, let's unpack the rest of our stuff from the car before Grandfather tries to do it himself."

The thick summer dark pressed around the porch lights, squeezing from them a dim yellow glow. All around him Jeff heard the rustle of leaves fat with full season's growth and the occasional flutter of night creatures. The air was warm and so soft against his skin that he felt he could lean into it and not fall. The house, its windows now bright with light, seemed safe and insulated from all unhappiness.

"Maybe there's nothing wrong with Grandfather at all," Jeff said into the receptive darkness. "Maybe he's just sorry we came home."

"Now, just a minute, Jeff." Mr. Armstead dropped the laundry bag and turned to face his son. "Your mother and I agree that we've got to clear up some things and set some ground rules with him. But that's only part of the problem. Your attitude's the other."

"But Dad," Jeff protested.

"Jeff, how do you think it makes your grandfather feel when you avoid him every chance you get? You cringe when he looks at you and mumble when he talks to you."

"I do?"

"Yes, you do. It's no wonder he glares at you. Half the time he can't even hear you. What's worse, you treat him like an outsider."

"Dad, you don't understand."

"You can't take his growl so personally. I know."

"I just want him to like me," Jeff said, surprising himself.

"Then stop acting as if *you* don't like *him*." His father stood looking at him, his lecture ended.

"All I really meant was, maybe Grandfather doesn't like being jammed in with us, any more than I do. Maybe he's just sorry that the week is over."

"I guess we all needed a break," Jeff's father said, more quietly. "Instant family hasn't suited your grandfather all that well."

"Maybe he misses his privacy. Wouldn't you? Maybe he likes being alone."

"He's been alone all his life, Jeff. That's why I was glad when he decided to come home. I expected all of us to make him feel welcome."

"I don't mean to make him feel bad."

"Any more than he means to nag you." The pale glow of the trunk light emphasized the lines in his face, and Mr. Armstead looked older, more like Grandfather. "I don't see any solution. He can't stay alone forever, even if he moves out now. But you and Megan can't share a room forever, either."

"We could get a bigger house, like Mom said."

"It would have to be a lot bigger to hold this crowd, bigger than a regional manager's salary can afford. Besides, Grandfather might not want to live with us anymore."

"Because of me?"

"He's got a lot on his mind right now, not just you. Try to remember that the next time he growls at you."

"I'll try, Dad."

"Now, let's get to work." He prodded the bag of dirty clothes with his toe. "That should go right down to the washing machine, and the fast food trash from the car goes in the garbage."

Jeff gathered up the loose napkins and milk shake cups from the car and shoved them into the greasy hamburger bag. Swinging it in one hand and dragging the laundry in the other, he started down the walk. He got as far as the front porch when the bag split open, raining packets of mustard and ketchup onto the ground.

"Rats," Jeff said, and flattened a bunch of the packets beneath the sole of his gym shoe. They exploded with a soft, satisfying sploot that sent streams of ketchup shooting into the air just as the screen door opened.

"But, Dad, we really ought to talk about this before you make a final decision," his mother was saying as she followed Grandfather onto the porch.

"There's nothing to discuss, Liz. I expected to be gone by the time you got back. Let's leave it at that."

Jeff's father looked up at the sound of their voices and saw Grandfather stop so abruptly that Mrs. Armstead stumbled into him. He seemed to stagger back and clutched at his chest.

"Dad?" Mr. Armstead dropped the suitcase and started to run for the stairs. "Dad, what's the matter? Are you all right?"

The red stain spread slowly down his shirt. Grandfather pulled his hand away and looked at the sticky, thick glob on his palm. Slowly, his head came up and he looked across the porch railing at Jeff.

"Ketchup," he said.

"You're all right?" Mr. Armstead stopped in midstride, straddling the lower two steps of the porch. He leaned back on the banister in relief. The suitcase tilted drunkenly on the walk behind him. "I thought you'd had some kind of a hemorrhage. What happened?"

Three pairs of eyes swiveled toward Jeff. He looked down, and lifted his foot off the squashed, now-empty packets. "I stepped on them."

"Five minutes, it didn't even take him five minutes," Jeff's father said to no one in particular, something like awe in his voice. Streaks of ketchup dribbled slowly down the white siding of the house, and clung in globs like June bugs to the screen.

Grandfather pulled a handkerchief from his pocket and began to dab at his face and hands. Mrs. Armstead ran her fingers through her hair suspiciously, but she had escaped the gooey flack.

"Jeffrey," she asked. "What is it with you and ketchup?"

"I'm sorry," Jeff said, amazed at the effect he'd achieved with one stamp of his foot. "I didn't know it would do that."

"What did you think it would do?" Grandfather stood beneath the porch light, his glasses glinting as he rubbed his hands on the handkerchief. "Did you think at all?"

"Probably not," Jeff's father said before Jeff could answer. And suddenly he began to laugh, shaking his head back and forth as he hung on the railing. "I wish I'd seen my face," he said, looking up at Grandfather. "I wish I'd seen your face. And Liz, look at the house!"

"My begonias," Jeff's mother said, bending over the flower boxes. "They're covered. Good thing they have red flowers." And she, too, began to laugh.

"Isn't anyone going to tell him he has to clean this up?" Grandfather asked. Firmly he controlled the twitching around his own mouth and forced a frown. "It's a mess."

"I know," Mr. Armstead said between gasps of laughter. He straightened and came up the stairs. "He's got his work cut out for him tomorrow. But you're all right, Dad, that's what matters. Give me that shirt and Jeff can take it downstairs with the rest of the laundry."

"After he picks up the rest of that garbage," Mrs. Armstead said. She bent over the railing to Jeff. "Please, just do what you're told. No more surprises tonight."

"Why would he do such a thing?" Jeff heard Grandfather ask as he dropped the trash into the garbage can.

"Why not?" Jeff's father returned and continued to chuckle. "You have to admit it was impressive, coming out of nowhere like that. Imagine if he'd done it to a perfect stranger in the middle of a McDonald's parking lot?"

"Why is that worse than doing it to someone he knows?"

"Because we're not perfect." The screen slammed on his father's laughter.

Twelve

It took Jeff most of the morning to scrub the dried ketchup off the shingles of the house and the porch and to spray the begonias clean. He didn't get to the laundry until nearly noon. Unloading the dryer for the third time, he carried his share upstairs and dumped it on his bed with the rest of his clean clothes.

He hated to fold shirts almost as much as he hated matching up socks. The shirts came out lumpy, and the socks, though they'd gone into the washer in twos, refused to pair up. In the old days he had a sock drawer and a shirt drawer, and what he pulled out, he wore. But since he and Megan had doubled up, he had to make room for both shirts and socks in one drawer. The only way to make sure he didn't get socks on his back and shirts on his feet was to fold them in separate stacks.

"Aren't you finished yet?" Megan poked her

head around the partition. "What a mess."

"Just beat it, Megan. Go away."

"I can't. Mom said to clean my room."

"It's not your room."

"It is, too. This half of it is. My stuff's put away."

Megan's bureau drawers were open, and her clean laundry was lined up in neatly folded piles. Her teddy bear sat squarely in the middle of her bed, and her slippers toed beneath it in perfect alignment. The comparison with Jeff's side was depressing.

"What's left to clean?" He began yanking socks out of the mound on his bed.

"Want some help?" Megan edged around to his side.

"I don't need any help." He didn't look up. "It's just that my clothes are bigger than yours so they take longer to fold."

Megan laughed and skipped over beside him. "When are we going back, Jeff?"

"To the lake? I don't know. I'm not going anywhere anytime soon."

"Not to the lake," Megan said, lowering her voice. "The house. When are we going back to the house?"

Jeff felt the weight of the key dragging at his pocket. "Forget it, Megan," he said, wishing she had. In the week at the lake the house had grown rather than diminished in his imagination. The more he tried not to think about it, the more often it came to mind. During the long ride home from the lake, the anticipation of seeing it again built until it was all Jeff could do not to ask his father to drive down Grove Street so he'd have a glimpse of the house as they passed.

"You don't want to go back there," he told Megan, in the vain hope that she'd agree. His own desire to return was strong enough for both of them, an urge he knew he couldn't continue to resist. It was like giving up chocolate, only worse. But he wanted to go back alone.

"You promised."

"I shouldn't have." Jeff tried to convince her. "We'll only get in trouble."

"You're just afraid I'll prove I'm right."

"I am not. I've got other stuff to do, that's all. Why can't you leave me alone? Who cares about your old house, anyhow? I haven't got time to fool with it."

Megan narrowed her eyes and set her mouth so that her face resembled a stubborn equals sign. "You promised we'd go back."

"We can't." Jeff sat down on his bed among the clean clothes and pulled Megan in front of him, eye to eye. "It's not our house. It's not magic. It doesn't have eyes or ears or a room for you."

"Prove it."

"Megan, I don't have to prove it. We don't own it. So we can't go inside."

"Then I'll go by myself." She jerked away from him and started out the door.

"Wait a minute." Jeff grabbed her arm. Her sudden independence confirmed his worst fears, that Megan couldn't be trusted to stay away, with or without him. "Don't you understand? We could be arrested."

"I don't care. What's arrested?"

"When you break the law, you get arrested. It's illegal to go into other people's houses."

"But my books are there, Jeff, and a room of my own. You'll see."

Jeff sighed. If he couldn't talk her out of it, he'd have to take her with him. "Even if I wanted to, we couldn't just sneak inside. We have to check it out first, to make sure no one moved in while we were away."

"When?"

"How should I know? I can't go anywhere right now. I don't have time, I told you."

"Mom said we could go to the park."

"When the chores were done." Jeff opened his arms to the heap around him. "Mine aren't. I'll be folding laundry until next week."

"Not if I help," Megan said. She began to smile. "We'll pass right by the house on the way to the park. It would only take a minute."

Jeff hesitated, torn between the desire to

visit the house immediately, even with Megan in tow, and the need to return alone, even if it meant waiting. He eyed his laundry, but the lure of the house was too great. "I guess it couldn't hurt just to take a look from the outside."

The two of them had the bed cleared in record time. Leaving a note for their mother, Jeff rode after Megan down Grove Street. At the archway in the hedge, she stopped.

"You go first," she said as Jeff pulled up beside her. Together they peered around the tall bushes. The yard and slate pathway were still ragged and untended. Jeff pushed his bike onto the lawn, where he couldn't be seen from the street. Megan followed, her orange flag waving above her head.

The long grass of the front lawn was bleached and dry. A sharp scent of bruised Queen Anne's lace rose from underfoot where they'd trampled on the low, fragile leaves. Everything was quiet, except for the hum of bees moving among the pink and white clover blossoms and dropping onto the white and yellow faces of wild daisies. Jeff scanned the house.

The front door was closed, but the plywood panel hung open on its hinges, and swung back against the shingles. Jeff strained to see some change in the place, some evidence of occupancy that hadn't been there a week ago.

To his immense relief, there was none. The porch still sagged on its rotted pilings, and the windows of the upper stories stared back at him as before, unshaded. Behind its high green hedge, the house cast shafts of light and shadow over the yard. They tingled on Jeff's shoulders, urging him gently forward.

"Can't we go closer?" Megan edged up to him. "We can't tell anything from here."

"It looks okay." Against his better judgment, but drawn by the house, Jeff began to wheel his bike down the drive. The stillness of the house and the weight of the key in his pocket carried him as far as the cellar door. He and Megan stood in the hot sun, staring at the bright silver lock.

"There's nobody here," Megan whispered. "We could run in quick and see my room."

"It wouldn't take long, would it?" Jeff was already rationalizing it to himself. If going inside convinced Megan that she had to stay away from the house, it was worth the chance they took. He didn't let himself think about returning to the house without her.

"Suppose Mom looks for us?" Now that Megan had gotten him this far, she lost her nerve. "We said we'd be at the park."

"And we will be, soon. You don't have to come if you don't want to. I'll tell you what I find."

But Megan shook her head. "No, if you're going, so am I."

"We'll look in your room and leave. No matter what's there, we aren't staying." He turned to make sure she agreed. "And then we'll go to the park."

Quickly they wheeled their bikes into the tent of honeysuckle beside the garage. Then Jeff and Megan sprinted across to the cellar door, opened the lock, and let themselves into the house. They stumbled as quietly as possible through the darkness to the stairs and tiptoed up into the kitchen. The worn linoleum crackled beneath their feet as they crept toward the dining room. Jeff held his finger to his lips.

"Don't say anything," he whispered. "We don't want anyone to hear us, if there is someone around."

Megan nodded, her eyes huge and black with excitement.

"Okay, come on then." Jeff pushed open the door and stepped into the dining room. Behind him he heard her gasp of disappointment. The far wall was still blank, only the dark oval outline of its absent painting marring the space. Jeff shushed her again, and led the way through the room to the hallway. Sunlight from the panes around the front door touched the figures on the Oriental runner, brightening the colors. Where the pattern faded again in the shadow of the stairway, Jeff stopped and took a deep breath. Megan reached for his hand. Slowly they climbed the stairs, easing from one to the next to avoid the creaking boards.

The stairs led to a wide landing. On either side of it were the closed doors that opened into the rooms of the second story. Toward the back of the house the hallway narrowed to accommodate another, enclosed stairway to the third floor, locked behind a heavy paneled door. At the opposite end, overlooking the front of the house, were two large windows, connected by a window seat. They had no shades, and light strained through their grimy panes onto the worn wooden floor.

"Your house's eyes don't look so lively from here, do they?" Jeff murmured. Megan shook her head and held onto his hand.

"Which one is mine?" she mouthed, looking from one door to the next.

"The turret room should be right here," Jeff whispered, pointing to the first door on the left. Together they crossed the landing and tried it. It stuck at first, then snapped free, squeaking slightly as it swung back to exhale a smell of fresh paint.

"Look, Jeff," Megan cried, awed into speech. "Now do you believe?"

The room was exactly as Megan had described it over the house phone. It had been painted a barely perceptible rose with white trim. The windows were hung, like the dining room's, with lace swags. Between them was a four-poster bed with a lace spread and canopy. A braided rag rug of many colors brightened the wood floor, dark with old layers of varnish. On one side of the room, set against the curving wall, was a small cradle. In it lay a baby doll with a delicately painted porcelain head and hands, dressed in a gown of lace, yellowed with age. On the other side was Megan's dollhouse.

In every detail it was the miniature of the house in which they stood. Its windows looked out like eyes from the second story. Beneath its porch was the front door bordered by panes of glass. The only difference between the houses, except for their size, was that the dollhouse was not in disrepair. There were curtains at its windows and furniture in its rooms.

"It's impossible," Jeff said. But Megan was already on her knees beside the house, opening the doors with their tiny knobs, cooing over the miniature wood stove in the kitchen and the replica canopy bed in the turret bedroom.

"It's magic, I told you." Megan grinned up at him. "This proves it."

"It doesn't prove anything. Lots of people would like this room. It's not magic, it's coincidence."

"There aren't any people," Megan said,

searching the small rooms. "Just like our big house, it hasn't any family."

"It's not our house, Megan." Jeff struggled to keep his voice at a normal level. "Stop saying that."

"Why is everything the way I asked, then?"

"I don't know." Jeff kept looking around the room for some clue. The depth of her conviction was beginning to frighten him. "But there has to be a reason."

"You said houses don't pick people, but this one did. That's why there's no family. We haven't moved in yet."

"Somebody's trying to trick us. It isn't magic." Jeff turned around and around in the curved room, his eyes moving from detail to detail until he was dizzy. He reached out and caught the doorknob for balance. "Let's get out of here."

For another minute Megan stayed on her knees, entranced by the dollhouse and the doll lying unrocked in its cradle. Then she stood up.

"I can play later, I guess," she said. "After I tell Mom."

"Are you crazy?" Jeff shouted at her. "You can't tell anyone."

"But it's our house, I know it is. She'll have to get ready to move in."

Jeff stared at her, truly alarmed. What had begun as one of Megan's harmless fantasies had become a nightmare. "Listen, Megan, it's all a mistake," he said softly, holding her by the shoulders. "I should never have come here, and I shouldn't have brought you."

"Don't worry, Jeff." She smiled up at him, her small face alight with pleasure. "Mom and Dad won't be mad, not after they see the house. There's so much room."

"But they can't see the house, not yet at least." Jeff tried to play for time. "We can't tell them yet, okay? Not until everything is in place, not until they have a room, too."

There was an explanation, there had to be, and he had to find it. But not now, not with Megan. He pointed her toward the door, and hurried after her onto the landing and down the stairs. He wanted them both out in the fresh air again, out of this strange and remarkable house.

They were on the bottom step when it happened. Cracking the hollow stillness, a voice engulfed them, trapping them where they stood on the open stair.

"Hi, folks," it said, innocently enough. But Jeff froze. His lungs, his heart, his entire chest seemed to lunge up into his throat. His hands and feet were suddenly cold, while his face burned, and sweat burst suddenly from pores he didn't know he had, running down his neck and the insides of his arms. He couldn't run. His knees were locked at a slippery distance from the rest of his body. But he could hear. Above the throbbing in his ears, over the rasping of his own breath, he heard the voice of the house.

"Greetings to you and to my Meg Ann from somewhere in war-torn Europe, as the correspondents say. It's cold and dark, and not much like Christmas, but a whole lot worse for those whose homes were bombed than for me. At least I know you're all safe and warm and full of turkey. I love you all . . . you all . . . you all. . . ."

There was a horrible scrape, like chalk on a blackboard, and then a click each time the words repeated themselves.

"What are you talking about?" Megan called out, before Jeff could stop her. She hopped down the last step and looked around the hall, poking her head into the dining room and parlor. "It's nowhere near Christmas, House."

Jeff clasped his hand over her mouth. "Be quiet," he whispered. From beyond the parlor the voice went on, over and over.

"It's not the house talking," he said. "I think it's a record. Just keep still till I find out."

He let her go and followed the sound from the hall to the parlor and into the library. A turntable was set on one of the shelves, and a small record was spinning beneath the needle arm. Jeff went over to it. With one finger he nudged the arm.

". . . you all . . . and I'll see you in six months, if all goes well." The voice lurched out of its groove and went on talking. "Whenever that seems too long a time, Miss Margaret, my Meg, step outside the library doors to the sundial. You can't imagine how often I think of that spot and the hours we spent there. Just remember that Time's shadow moves as slowly for me here as it does for you there, but it is moving. I'll be home to keep the promises I made you, if you'll still have me. We'll celebrate in June all the holidays we missed, and still have a lifetime of holidays ahead of us. Think of me. Stay well, and have a happy New Year."

Silence. Only the soft sweep of the needle across the final threads of the recording disturbed the abrupt quiet. Jeff lifted the needle and shut off the machine. He stared at the yellow blur of the label as it slowed and came into focus. The record drifted to a stop and he read the inscription. "USO — 1945."

"Who was that?" Megan stood on tiptoe beside him to look at the record. "Was he talking to me?"

"It was some other Meg." As Jeff looked up to answer, a flash of light from the still shuttered bay window distracted him. A narrow French door, unnoticeable before behind the panel of protective plywood, swung open in a current of fresh air. Jeff blinked, but it was no illusion. The scent of sun-warmed grass was in the room.

"Wait, stop," Jeff called out and rushed to the door. But he was not quick enough. Outside the patio was empty and still. "Come back. Who are you?"

There was no answer. Jeff stood alone in the brick patio he'd found on his first visit to the house. It was still and silent behind its border of azaleas, except for the vibration of a single rhododendron branch close to the house. It scraped against the boards that had been left leaning up on the clapboard siding. A pile of new bricks was stacked nearby, and the overgrown bushes had been hacked back in a graceful half circle. At its center, overlooked by moss-covered concrete benches, was the repaired sundial, its broken metal face mended to catch the shadow of the sun.

Jeff went back inside. His head buzzed as if he'd hung too long upside down from the beech tree and permanently inverted his perception of things.

"Jeff," Megan demanded, tugging at his arm. "Answer me. What other Megan?"

"Not Megan, Margaret, I think. But he called her Meg, like a nickname. 'My Meg,' he said." Jeff crossed the room. "Where's that book you found?"

"My fairy tales?" Megan ran over to the bookshelf and pulled the volume from its place. She flipped it open and held it out to Jeff.

"*Meg Ann S.*" he saw, written in childish but careful script among the flourishes of the bookplate design. "It is your name, sort of, but not your book. It belongs to that other Meg Ann, the one who lived here years ago."

"You mean she's come back?" Megan's eyes widened even further. "Has she come back as a ghost to haunt the house?"

"Ghosts don't do brickwork or paint walls," Jeff said. "Besides, though she'd be pretty old by now, she wouldn't necessarily be a ghost."

"But why would an old lady want fairy tales and a dollhouse?" Megan took the book back. "They may have been hers, but the house wants me to have them now."

Looking around the room, Jeff could almost believe it. The changes in the house were not modern improvements. People who restored old houses put new appliances in the kitchen and whirlpool tubs in the bathroom, not dollhouses in the bedroom and sundials in the garden. The house had come alive for him and for Megan with enticements of a simpler kind, the kind that could turn it into a home. It was as if the house, awakened from its dusty stillness, had claimed them for its own, to share in its new life.

"Why just you?" Jeff asked Megan. "If the

house is really magic, it should know what we all need. If it's ours, where's my room? And one for Mom and Dad?"

"You haven't asked." Grabbing his arm, Megan tried to tug him to the house phone in the kitchen. But Jeff stood firm. His eye fell again on the open French door, swung back to the fresh air of the garden, still trembling from the touch of whoever had rushed out through it.

"If it were magic, I wouldn't have to ask. There'd be a room for me with drawers and shelves for all my stuff, and a desk where I could work on my models. I'd have all the space I wanted. We wouldn't smell paint. The walls would just turn blue. There'd be a studio for Mom, and maybe even a shop for Dad."

His words rang out in the hollow library, bouncing off the empty shelves, and echoing like whispered answers from floor to ceiling, rippling into the closed rooms of the house.

"Something's going on here," Jeff said. "But whatever it is, it isn't magic."

His own words came back to them, half heard in the shimmering space. "Magic, magic, magic."

Thirteen

Fully dressed, Jeff lay in bed with the covers pulled up under his chin. It was hot, and the sheet stuck to his neck, but it hid his T-shirt and jeans. Until his parents made their nightly check, he had no choice. He'd just have to swelter.

Mr. and Mrs. Armstead turned the TV off and the dishwasher on. Above its crescendo Jeff heard them climb the stairs and stop for a moment outside Grandfather's room. Since the night they arrived home from the lake, when his parents had sat up late arguing with Grandfather, he had kept to himself. Jeff heard the worry in the low murmur of his parents' voices as they left Grandfather undisturbed and entered the children's room.

Jeff pulled the sheet closer around his neck and jammed his head under the pillow. Footsteps stopped beside his bed. His mother slipped past the partition to straighten Megan's covers and smooth her thick, dark curls. Jeff clutched his sheet in both fists and waited.

"How can he sleep that way in this heat?" His mother's hand fell lightly on his shoulder. "You'd think he'd suffocate."

"Leave him alone," his father said. "He'll come out from under if he's too warm."

They went out, leaving the door open to whatever currents stirred the night air. After a long time the lamp in their room went out. Only the glow of light from Grandfather's room remained. Jeff couldn't remember his ever checking on his grandchildren, and he couldn't wait any longer. From under his pillow Jeff pulled his wilted, wrinkled note. If he didn't get back by morning, he didn't want his parents to think he'd run away or, worse, that he'd simply disappeared into the hot July night.

Slipping sideways out of bed, he lumped the pillow into a vaguely human shape, put the note on top of it, and covered it all with the sheet. From under his bed he dragged his sneakers, the laces tied together, and slung them around his neck. For a moment he crouched beside the bed, listening. All was still. He began to crawl toward the open window.

Only a sliver of moon lit the night sky. Snatches of bark gleamed through the leaves of the white birch. Languid with the heat, its branches drooped low to the ground. Jeff slid the screen up and stepped through the window onto the porch roof. His socks caught on the rough shingle as he edged his way toward the tree. At the corner of the porch he paused, measuring the distance, and then jumped. He was hanging from the limb when he heard another scrabble across the shingle. He swung down from the tree onto the lawn.

"Jeff, wait for me."

"You can't come." He saw her dark hair outlined against the white clapboard of the house. "You really can't come this time, Megan."

"Come where?" She stood just above him on the roof, her hands on her hips. "Where are you going?"

"To catch your magic. Go back to bed."

"I'm coming with you."

"You can't," Jeff whispered, but his voice sounded loud in the still, humid air. "I have to do this by myself."

"I come, or we both stay. Take me with you or I'll shout for Mom and Dad." She opened her mouth to yell.

"All right," Jeff said, waving both arms to shush her. "Come on then. But you'll have to keep up. And be quiet."

The birch tree rustled as Megan climbed into its branches. A moment later she dropped beside him, still wearing her pajamas and slippers. Jeff shoved his feet into his sneakers and tied them without looking at her, and led the way off through the backyards toward Grove Street.

Everything was noisier at night. With every step he was sure they'd be stopped by parents or neighbors. Twigs cracked, gravel crunched, and dogs barked loudly enough to wake every family on the block. At the corner, pulling Megan with him, Jeff held his breath and plunged across the unsheltered spaces where they might be seen by passing motorists. How could he explain what he was doing at midnight dragging his little sister in her pajamas down the street to a vacant, run-down ruin of a house? He darted through the arched hedge at last and slid to the ground to catch his breath.

"Now what?" Megan asked, still panting.

Jeff's mouth and throat were dry, and he had to swallow two or three times before he could talk. "There's something funny about all this," he said. "The changes in the house happen in secret. There aren't any trucks or workmen here during the day, the way there should be if someone were moving in."

"I told you. Then you *do* believe it's our house." Megan's sudden smile flashed white in the shadow. "Why else would there be a room for me?"

"That's what I'd like to know, and I'm about to find out."

"You're going inside at night? Alone?" Megan's face tilted toward him, now a blurred and worried glimmer.

"I told you not to come."

"I'm not scared."

"It's too late even if you are. You can't stay out here by yourself. You'll have to come with me." Jeff wiped the sweat off his face with the tail of his shirt and stood up. Across the yard the house loomed above them, visible only as a block of denser darkness against the sky. "At least no one's inside yet. We can sneak in and take our position."

"Take it where? What position?"

"For spying," Jeff said. If Megan's presence did nothing else, it forced him to state his plans. Saying them out loud reassured him and made everything sound almost plausible. Besides, she was someone to talk to. He didn't like to think about how he would have felt, creeping alone in the shadow of the house, preparing to confront its magician.

"Hang on to my shirt so we don't get separated," he told her. "We can't take the chance of turning on lights and being seen."

Under cover of the hedge they skirted the house and crept back along its south wall to the cellar door. The thick branches of rhododendron creaked above them, rattling at the slightest touch. A musty odor of compost rose from the rotting leaves wedged in their roots. Jeff and Megan ducked through the darkness, swathed in shadows thick and dark and warm as a black woolen cloak. At the hatch Jeff stopped and knelt on the slanted door, feeling for the lock. The metal was slippery in his sweaty hand, and he couldn't see the numbers on the dial. Blindly he rotated the knob.

"Jeff, someone's coming!" Megan jerked so hard on his shirt that she nearly toppled him over. He felt the lock give way as the hasp snapped open. Glancing over his shoulder, Jeff saw the light moving just inside the hedge, coming toward them down the driveway.

"Quick, before he sees us." Jeff urged Megan through the open hatchway. He slipped in after her, and pulled the cover down behind them.

The cellar was blacker than ever. They huddled at the bottom of the steps, staring up at the tiny slit between the slanted doors, waiting for it to brighten as the light came closer. They heard the crunch of gravel first, then a pause and muttered exclamation as the light steadied on the door. Suddenly the hatch opened in a flash of brightness and thudded closed again. Jeff heard the click of the lock, the rattle of metal as it fell back against the latch.

"He locked us in." Megan clutched his arm. "We can't get out."

Jeff couldn't see her face. He felt the warm, panicked puff of her words on his cheek and the points of her small fingers in his arm. "It's all right," he whispered. "There's the front door and the library door. We'll get out."

"But he knows we're here. He'll find us."

"Maybe, maybe not," Jeff said, thinking fast. "He might believe he forgot to lock the hatch himself. And even if he does know we're here, he doesn't know where we are. It's a big house. We can hide. But we have to hurry, Megan, and get out of here before he locks the kitchen door, too."

She needed no encouragement. The last place either one of them wanted to spend the night was in the cellar. Megan's breath wheezed in Jeff's ear as they bumped along the path to the stairs. Casting about with both hands to avoid collisions, Jeff led the way as fast as he could. Megan's slippers rasped behind him on the dirt-encrusted floor. Jeff tried not to hear the faint rustle and squeak above their heads and the swift pattering of rodents among the boxes to either side. At last they reached the stairs and tumbled awkwardly up to the door.

No light showed yet around its edges. Jeff turned the knob and pushed. It swung back, letting him and Megan into the kitchen. She fell back against the door while Jeff locked the dead bolt.

"Safe," she breathed.

"Not yet," Jeff said. "We have to hide."

But in the dining room Megan stopped again.

"The painting is hung." She skidded to a halt behind Jeff and pulled back on his shirt. "Wait, I have to see it. Can't you shine the flashlight, just once?"

Jeff looked up, and he, too, stopped. The oval portrait hung at last at the head of the table, and even in the shadows he recognized that face.

"That's me," Megan said, running over to it and peering up. "Who could have painted a picture of me?"

"It isn't you. She's much older than you. It's just somebody with the same color hair and eyes." But he knew it was more than that. The woman in the picture looked down at him with Megan's smile out of the same-shaped face. Though her hair was pulled back in an old-fashioned chignon, tendrils of curls escaped and brushed her cheeks and neck as Megan's did.

"We don't have time to talk about it now. Come on."

Catching her hand, Jeff pulled her away from the portrait toward the hall. Here the darkness was lifting. Through the glass panes of the front door the beam of a flashlight showed. In a moment the doorway gleamed with light. The old boards of the porch creaked with the weight of footsteps. Dragging Megan beside him, Jeff ran up the stairs. They were on the landing when they heard the front door open and close and saw the shaft of light touch the Oriental rug and the foot of the stairs before it moved into the dining room.

"Your room," Jeff whispered, and shoved Megan ahead of him into the turret room. "You'll be safe here."

"Don't leave me alone." Megan's whisper trembled with tears. "I want to stay with you."

"Trust me, Megan." He flattened her against the wall, so that when the door opened, she would be hidden behind it. "Once he looks here, he won't come back. Stay behind the door and he won't see you. And if he does, I'll distract him so you can get away."

"But I'm scared."

"Me, too, but there's nothing else to do. You're safe in your own room. And I'll be right outside, in the window seat." Jeff forced a grin, and squeezed her hand. "I have to see what he does. Don't worry. You'll be all right."

He darted back to the landing before she could argue, closing the door behind him. Downstairs light flowed from the dining room into the hallway. Diamond patterns glittered off the chandelier onto the carpet at the foot of the stairs, but Jeff didn't pause to examine them. He climbed into the window seat and dropped the lid, leaving only a crack open to the landing. He heard the heavy tread on the stairs and saw the light moving up toward them. Jeff could make out no more than a dark shape. It came inexorably onward, opening the door of each room, glancing inside, and then, to Jeff's horror, closing and locking each one. Jeff could do nothing but watch as the footsteps approached Megan's room, paused, and opened the door.

The flashlight swung up from the floor and pierced the turret room, then dropped again. The figure hesitated, then followed the light across the threshold. Jeff poised to leap out of his hiding place and tackle whoever it was. But before he could move, the person reappeared and closed the door firmly. Through his spyhole Jeff saw a key slipped into the lock of Megan's door, and heard the bolt shoot home. Passing within inches of the window seat, the figure turned, pocketing the keys, and continued on around the landing toward the rear of the house.

The light dimmed, and Jeff was left in complete darkness. Behind her locked door, Megan was absolutely still. Digging his fingers into his wrist, Jeff counted the minutes by the beat of his pulse. When he reached five hundred and still heard nothing, he eased up the lid of the window seat and crawled out.

The moon was at its height and cast a faint glow through the blank eyes of the second-story windows. Jeff squinted down the dark hall and saw only the closed doors. He edged over to Megan's and pressed his mouth to the crack at the doorway.

"Megan, it's me. Are you all right? Come to the door." He heard the rustle of movement and the scrape of her slippers.

"I want to go home." She struggled not to sob. "Can't we go home, Jeff?"

"In a little while. There's something I have to do first. You're safe there now. The door is locked." He listened to her smothered sniffs beyond the door and hoped she wouldn't demand to be let out, not yet. "I'll come back before you know it. Be brave. Just climb in bed, Megan, and wait for me."

"All right, but hurry." She sounded doubtful, but he heard her move away from the door.

"Are you in bed?"

"Yes, and guess what, Jeff?" Her voice was suddenly light, the thickness of tears thinned by surprise. "My teddy bear is here. The house had my bear right here on the bed."

"That's . . . that's great," Jeff said, swallowing hard. He pressed his hand against the solid wood of the door as if that could guarantee her safety and tried not to think about what he'd gotten them into. "You just snuggle up with your bear, then, and wait for me."

As he straightened up, he looked out at the front lawn. An entire chunk of it was visible, touched by a light from the top of the house. It seemed to originate in the turret, from the third-floor room directly above Megan's. Jeff knew now where the figure had gone. He turned and ran down the hall to the closed stairway, grabbed the knob, and pulled. The door was locked. As Jeff fell on it, determined to tear it down if necessary, a solid object jabbed sharply at his hip. He yanked the heavy shanked key from his pocket and fitted it into the lock. The bolt shot back, and Jeff opened the door.

The stairs wound steeply upward into rooms piled with furniture beneath sloped ceilings. Light streamed into them from a doorway on the right. Dangling from its keyhole was a ring of keys. Jeff tiptoed toward it, edging along the wall. From inside he could hear a soft, regular sweeping, and a sticky, snapping sound. As he crept closer, he recognized the smell of paint.

So the magician is working his wonders on the other turret room, Jeff thought, and slipped up to the door. Stretching with his right hand while he balanced himself with his left, Jeff reached out for the key ring, easing it from the lock with the tips of his fingers, tilting it slowly into his palm.

With a crash it fell, hitting the wood floor in a jangle of metal. Jeff snatched for it, felt his hand close on it, as a rough palm came down on his neck and dragged him forward into the light.

"So there you are!" the gruff voice said. The hand propelled him across the room and deposited him on a low stool opposite the door. "I've got you now."

Fourteen

"And none too soon, either," the voice went on. "No telling what kind of mischief you'd have been into next."

Jeff blinked as his eyes adjusted to the sudden bright light. Slowly the figure blocking the doorway came into focus — the stained overalls and spattered shirt, the stiff-billed cap and worn work boots, the gnarled hands flecked with blue paint.

"Grandfather? It's you?"

"Who did you expect?"

"You locked us in the cellar?"

"I had to keep you here somehow. It was the only way to make sure you didn't leave once you got in." Grandfather frowned and tipped his head so that the light glinted from his glasses. "Just what did you think you were doing, sneaking out in the dead of the night, dragging your sister along with you?"

"She wasn't supposed to come. I told her not to."

"A lot of good that did. Didn't it occur to you that it was wrong, even dangerous?" Grandfather's bushy eyebrows lowered in a fierce line above his eyes. "You might have been hurt."

"If we weren't scared to death first," Jeff said, as relief and then anger replaced shock. "How could you do that to us?"

"It was for your own good," Grandfather said in his stern growl. "Suppose it hadn't been your grandfather who caught you?"

"But it was. Couldn't you have told us, instead of locking Megan all alone in that room?" Jeff stood up and found his knees were still too wobbly for sudden movements. "I have to tell her everything's all right."

"Sit down. She's asleep." Grandfather nodded toward a small speaker near the door. "If you listen you can hear her breathing."

"An intercom? You mean the house is wired?"

"Something like that," Grandfather said. "I switched it on as soon as I got up here. She fell asleep talking to her bear just after you left her."

"You did that, too, brought her teddy bear from home."

"Both your beds were empty. It didn't take

much imagination to figure out where you'd gone." Grandfather's frown deepened. "It was time we had a talk, you and I."

"You locked all the doors. How could we talk if I never found you?"

"You had the key, the only key you needed. I waited here, behind the one door you could open." He watched Jeff slip the brass key ring out of his pocket. "Where did you find it?"

"In the backyard," Jeff said, turning it over on his palm. "It must have been there for a hundred years. I found it in the tomato patch."

"Where I dropped it." Grandfather pulled his pocket inside out to show Jeff the hole. "I've carried that key with me for over thirty years and never lost it once, until now. And you found it."

He looked directly at Jeff, peering over the silver frame of his glasses. Vertical lines cut deeply into his cheeks, and a fan of small creases opened out around his eyes. They were still frosty blue, but the sharp edge was gone from his voice.

"I'd say that means something, wouldn't you? You must be lucky."

"You're the one who gave me the four-leaf clover," Jeff said, slowly looking from the key to Grandfather.

"So I did," the old man said, in the same quiet tone. Then his lips tightened into their familiar frown. "You took some big chances with that key."

"I was going to give it back," Jeff protested. "That's why I came here in the first place, to find out who lived here."

"And in the second place?" Grandfather asked.

"Megan insisted." Honesty won out, and Jeff blurted, "But I'd have come back anyway. I had to."

"I see." Grandfather nodded slowly. "You should have told your parents what you were doing."

"Why didn't you? You knew we were here." Suddenly the obvious struck Jeff. "What are you doing here?"

"Working," Grandfather said, opening his hands to take in the room.

"This house is yours?" Finally the pieces came together, in an incomplete picture, with gaps and yawning rents, but at last comprehensible. "This is the property you had to settle."

Grandfather nodded.

"Then you did all this. You're Megan's magician."

"No magic involved, just hard work."

"Megan doesn't know that. She thinks it's magic. She thinks the house is ours." Jeff's anger flared. "You made her think that. She wouldn't have wanted to come back here otherwise. Why blame me for bringing her here when it's your fault she wanted to come, not mine?"

"Because you should have had better sense than to come here at night." He glared at Jeff.

"I've got better sense than to fix up a room to fool some little kid," Jeff said, defending himself. "You did fix it for her, didn't you?"

"The dollhouse and the doll were your grandmother's." Light winked off Grandfather's glasses as he spoke. "Doing what Megan asked seemed harmless enough, since it had to be done in any case before the house could be sold."

"Sold? You can't sell it," Jeff cried. "Please, Grandfather, not now. Megan thinks that room is hers. She'd never understand. She thinks the house is alive."

"She's not far wrong. It does come alive when you're here." The thought of Megan seemed to soften the old man. He looked down at his hands. He rubbed his rough, swollen knuckles in silence for a moment, smearing the spatters of paint into streaks. When he looked up, he gave Jeff a short nod that bestowed a measure of approval and respect. "You wouldn't be any more satisfied than I would be with less than the whole story. But I'll have to talk and work at the same time if I'm going to get this job done tonight."

He filled the roller with paint and faced the wall. For a long moment he stared at it, and then rolled a huge M of paint and began.

"Your grandmother's people owned this house, the Stratton family. They had everything I did not — money, position, land, and Margaret Ann." He paused, filled in a space, and went on.

"Some people have a knack for life. They brighten everything around them. She was like that, Meg was. Not like you and me, who go at things straight on, like battering rams. She was like a hummingbird. She had lightness."

"Like Megan," Jeff said.

Grandfather shot him a glance over his shoulder and nodded. "She had the same kind of determination as our Megan, too. So when she decided to marry me, there was no changing her mind. And her parents tried. But like Megan, she'd decided. I blessed my luck and never questioned it."

"That's her in the picture downstairs, isn't it?" Jeff asked. "She looks like Megan."

The old man nodded. "If it hadn't been for your sister, I'd never have looked at that picture again. I'd forgotten how beautiful she was."

He paused to clear his throat. Jeff waited while he removed his glasses and swabbed the lenses with a big red handkerchief.

"Finally the Strattons agreed to a wedding. They had no choice, really. But they couldn't give Meg up entirely, and who could blame them? I was too happy not to be generous." He bent down and dipped the roller in the paint, squatting over it as he talked.

"When Mr. Stratton offered us a place to live, I accepted. With housing scarce after the war, it would have been difficult to refuse. He converted the servants' quarters here in the attic into an apartment for us. This room was my study. Meg Ann and I moved in and were happy. We were still living here when your father was born."

Again he paused, and again Jeff waited.

"After she died, I couldn't raise him myself. It was my Meg who had a way with people, not I. I couldn't even stay in this town. Without her it was an empty world. So I packed up our things, left Gene with Aunt Dorf, and ran." He looked over at Jeff. "I ran away. I'm not proud of it, but that's what I did. I never expected to see this place again or to care about anyone in it."

"But you did come back."

"Expectations are not guarantees." He pursed his lips, and resumed his story, as if he'd memorized it and could only tell it in a certain way.

"The Strattons rented the house out after old Mr. Stratton died, and the family moved away. I guess they couldn't stand it here without Meg anymore than I could. But then the tenants moved on, and it was too big for most families, so it sat vacant for years, until the last of the Strattons died last spring."

"That's why you came back to Arborton."

"That was part of it. The rest doesn't matter now." Grandfather stood up and turned his back on Jeff. Carefully he smoothed the stripes of blue evenly on the wall. "I planned to sell the house as it stood, without ever going inside. I would have, too, if it hadn't been for you."

"Me? What did I do?"

"Made me face facts, for one thing," Grandfather answered, his tone as smooth and even as the paint. But Jeff could see how his lower jaw tightened, and the lines around his mouth folded heavily downward. "You left me no doubt that I didn't belong here, not in your family."

Jeff ducked his head, though he couldn't dodge the words.

"It was your father's idea that I come to stay, and I should have known it wouldn't work. I'm a bad-tempered old man," Grandfather said in the same flat tone. "I don't know anything about families. I never did, and in spite of what your father thinks, I'm too old to learn."

The roller of paint went up and down, filling the zigzags on the wall, its sticky splat the only sound in the room. It seemed louder in the silence between them, drowning out their breathing and the soft rustle of Grandfather's worn denims.

"The only logical place to stay was here, until it was sold. I made some arrangements for light and water, then forced myself to come take a look around. It was quite a surprise when some prospective tenants showed up."

"You mean Megan and me? How did you know it was us?"

"You left some clues, and that orange flag on Megan's bike is hard to miss. I was up here taking inventory the day you discovered the house phone," Grandfather said. He motioned with his free hand toward the other rooms. "It connects with the servants' quarters, remember. I recognized your voices."

"So when Megan spoke to the house, she was really talking to you."

"That's right. I heard every word." He paused and stepped back from the wall. "All our things were packed away up here. I simply put them downstairs where they belonged."

"The furniture was already in the dining room," Jeff said, thinking over the changes. "You cleaned it up and left my grandmother's books on the shelves for Megan to find. But our initials were on the napkin rings."

"Margaret Stratton Armstead was her name." Grandfather looked out the skylight at the sprinkling of stars, seeing memories beyond Jeff's reach. "MSA and JCA, for Jeffrey Charles Armstead," he explained, and turned to face Jeff. "You are my namesake, you know."

Jeff nodded. It was all so simple, so clear, that he wondered why he had not seen it from the beginning. "You put the new lock on the cellar and took the panel off the front door. You left the sandwiches and cookies for me and Megan, and the flowers."

"Your grandmother liked flowers."

"So does Megan. You went to a lot of trouble."

Grandfather stooped down over the paint pan. "I rather enjoyed it."

"You knew we'd come back. That's why you left the key out."

"I wanted you to like the house." He concentrated on wetting the roller. "Until you two began to fuss over it, I'd forgotten what it was like."

"And the voice in the library? That was you, too."

"It was." Grandfather pushed himself up, straightening his back by degrees. "Not that you could recognize that young man as this old grouch."

Hearing his own description from Grandfather's lips made Jeff wince. Even if it was the truth, he wished he hadn't said it aloud, where Grandfather could overhear him. He stared in mute apology at the broad back, bent and stiff beneath the denim shirt. Megan would know what to say. She would make Grandfather feel better. She would make him laugh, and the cold glint of his glasses would become a mere sparkle in his face. Jeff could only watch and listen.

"I had my life ahead of me then," Grandfather said. "I'd been sent overseas at the end of World War II, and Meg and I were planning to get married when I got home. We resented having to wait, but nothing made me appreciate home the way those months in the rubble of Europe did. I found the record while I was getting this room ready." He stared at the painted wall. "You nearly had me that day. If Megan hadn't shouted, I wouldn't have had time to get out through the patio."

"You interrupted the record. There was a scrape, and it started repeating itself."

"I decided I didn't want to hear it after all." Grandfather put the roller down and began to wipe his hands on his handkerchief.

"But I played it through." Jeff took a deep breath and plunged. "I'm sorry, Grandfather."

The creases deepened around Grandfather's mouth, but he looked only sad, not angry. He kept wiping his hands, looking down at the knobby knuckles, rubbing the cloth carefully over his nails. Finally he lifted his head to face Jeff squarely.

"I'm glad you played it. It was good for me. It made me realize how different my life could have been." He cleared his throat, but his voice still sounded thick and choked. "Because of you I've replaced a bitter sadness with other, happier memories. I can leave here now. I want to thank you for that."

"I didn't exactly plan it," Jeff said awkwardly. Grandfather's thanks was the last thing he expected. It surprised and embarrassed him. "But I'm glad," he added.

Grandfather nodded. "I thought you might be. You've made it possible for me to leave here now."

"But you just said you were staying." Jeff pushed up off the stool, crashing it over behind him as he stood up. "You can't sell the house and leave, Grandfather, don't you understand? You have to stay, for Megan at least. You can't take her room away from her, not when you've made her think it's hers."

"You really think I'd do that? To Megan or to you?" His mouth set again in a thin line. "Don't you like this room? Is there something wrong with the color? No sense my going on with it if you don't like it."

"Why should you care what I like? What difference does that make?"

"You'll have to live with it."

"It's mine?" Jeff stared in astonishment. In his daydream, and now in reality, the owner of the house was offering him a room of his own. The room above Megan's in the turret mirrored hers in shape. But against these walls Grandfather had fashioned curving shelves from floor to ceiling and deep cabinets beneath each window. There was a loft bed, with a drafting table and stool beneath it. Opposite the door was a skylight, a movable slab of glass with a telescope in front of it. Slowly Jeff took it all in. Even in the clutter of paint cans and brushes and rags, he could see that thought and effort had gone into the design of the room. He turned in a complete circle until he faced Grandfather again.

"You did this for me?"

"A boy needs a place of his own."

"But why? You don't even like me."

Grandfather didn't answer for a moment. He slipped off his glasses and rubbed the bridge of his nose. "I thought it was the other way around."

His eyes held Jeff's, bright blue and distant, yet familiar. Without glasses they were very much like Jeff's own.

"Because I can't live in the same house with you, Jeffrey, doesn't mean I don't like you."

"You can live with Megan. You get along fine with her."

"Megan's like your grandmother."

"And I'm like you." Unconsciously Jeff thrust out his jaw. "Dad says I take after you."

"He's right enough about that." Grandfather

blinked, and the corners of his eyes crinkled into deep webs, but his mouth remained firm. "You're a real Armstead, all right, too independent and stubborn by half. There's room for only one of those in any family. You'll get along fine without me."

"But this is your house."

"And it needs a family, Jeffrey, but the family doesn't need me. I've turned it upside down. Your mother can't paint, your father does nothing but try to keep the peace, and I can't even pass you the milk without starting World War III." His jaw was set like Jeff's, but his voice was soft. "That's my fault, not yours. As soon as I finish here, I'm leaving."

"No, you can't." To his dismay Jeff's voice cracked, but he kept on. "If Dad can't divorce me, you can't divorce him. You're stuck with us."

"You don't want an old grouch like me around," Grandfather said. "It's better that I go."

"That's just running away again. Besides, if I'm too young for the Peace Corps, you must be too old. Where would you go?" The words came all in a rush, as though saying enough of them fast enough would allow Jeff to say the right ones. They spread between him and Grandfather like the pale stain of blue on the walls, covering the stark white spaces of their anger with the hope of understanding. "Isn't there room here for all of us?" Jeff asked uncertainly.

"I wouldn't change just because the house is bigger."

"I wouldn't, either." Jeff's blue eyes met the frosty old ones. "Maybe you could have the apartment again, and we could live in the rest of the house."

"I don't know if I can be part of a family," Grandfather said, doubt shading his voice. In that instant Jeff saw a different man. This was no magician, not even the strict and distant grandfather he'd learned to avoid. This was an old man reaching out for one last chance at something he thought he'd lost forever.

"Could you try?" Jeff wasn't sure he wanted to hear the answer, but he knew he had to ask the question. Invite him in and he won't have to bang the door down, his father had said.

"Could you?" Grandfather asked him. "I'd be right next to your room. You wouldn't like that." He hesitated. "Of course you could always lock the door. And you don't have to take this room."

Grandfather stood very still. His shoulders were stiff with a tension that stretched down his arms and tightened his knuckles in a white grip on the handkerchief. His hands trembled, and he shoved his glasses back on his nose. Suddenly it seemed very important to Jeff to loosen that tightness.

"I could try."

Grandfather coughed. "Then so could I."

"I'd like to have this room," Jeff said into the sudden silence, in the most businesslike voice he could muster. "I really need the space, and the shelves."

"You'll have to learn to use that telescope properly." Grandfather issued the order in the old gruff voice, but Jeff was no longer offended by it.

"Then you'll have to teach me." He snapped back his own order, matching Grandfather chin for chin and eye for eye. For a moment they balanced opposite each other in the pale blue room. Then Jeff grinned. Like some creaky mechanism long unused, Grandfather's mouth edged into a grin of its own that mirrored Jeff's.

"I'll try," he said.

Jeff held out his hand, gripping Grandfather's calloused palm, folding his fingers around the thick joints, sealing their compact. As if galvanized by the contact, Grandfather pulled him close, and for a bare instant Jeff was pressed against the soft denim of Grandfather's overalls, Grandfather's arm tight around him. Just as suddenly they broke apart, and stood at arm's length in the ring of the newly painted turret room.

"We'd better collect Megan and get you two home to bed."

"I'm ready if you are, Grandfather," Jeff said. He ventured a smile. "Let's all go home."

About the Author

JAN O'DONNELL KLAVENESS wrote her first book, *A Funny Girl Like Me*, for Scholastic. She is also the author of *The Griffin Legacy, Ghost Island*, and *Keeper of the Light*.

Beyond the Cellar Door began as a short story about a Victorian house in Sea Cliff, New York, that intrigued Ms. Klaveness. The story then grew into a novel as she explored the relationship between grandparents and grandchildren, and the uncanny ability of many youngsters to discover a person's true character, even through a prickly exterior.

Jan Klaveness lives in Hempstead, New York, and has two children.